"I'm going to keep the baby. I'll raise it myself."

He couldn't be serious, yet apparently he was. "What brought you to this astounding conclusion?"

The planes of Lock's face softened. When his mouth curved tenderly, Erica remembered with a pang how he'd gazed at her on the night they'd made love.

Which is how we got into this mess.

"Knowing that you're carrying our baby, becoming a daddy, well, it's the most wonderful thing that's ever happened to me. I can't give that up."

The devotion on his face sent an intense yearning through Erica. For an instant, she wondered what it would be like to create a family with Lock and the baby.

To have a home instead of feeling like a perpetual outsider.

Dear Reader,

It's often said that opposites attract, but interesting relationships can also arise when characters have too much in common.

That's what I discovered while writing the story of Erica and Lock. At first, I struggled with the idea that both were dealing with the same kind of abandonment issues and self-protective behavior. Then I realized that their similarities presented intriguing obstacles that they had to overcome together.

For those of you new to the Safe Harbor Medical miniseries, don't worry about what you've missed, because each book stands on its own. For those who've read some or all of the earlier half-dozen books, I hope you'll enjoy seeing familiar faces.

Dr. Owen Tartikoff, hero of *The Surgeon's Surprise Twins*, is back in a supporting role, since Erica works as his surgical nurse. Also, senior Renée Green, a hospital volunteer who first appeared in that book, now assumes a more significant role. I don't want to give away too much, but keep your eye on her.

You'll also encounter secondary characters who'll take center stage in future books, including detective Mike Aaron, Dr. Paige Brennan and Dr. Zack Sargent. As for sarcastic anesthesiologist Rod Vintner, I may just keep him around as an entertaining counterpoint, but who knows?

Welcome to Safe Harbor, or welcome back! It's great to have you here.

Best,

Jacqueline Diamond

The Detective's Accidental Baby

JACQUELINE DIAMOND

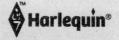

TORONTO NEW YORK LONDON
AMSTERDAM PARIS SYDNEY HAMBURG
STOCKHOLM ATHENS TOKYO MILAN MADRID
PRAGUE WARSAW BUDAPEST AUCKLAND

Recycling programs
for this product may
not exist in your area.

ISBN-13: 978-0-373-75396-3

THE DETECTIVE'S ACCIDENTAL BABY

Copyright © 2012 by Jackie Hyman

This edition published by arrangement with Harlequin Books S.A.

For questions and comments about the quality of this book
please contact us at Customer_eCare@Harlequin.ca

www.Harlequin.com

Printed in U.S.A.

ABOUT THE AUTHOR

A former reporter and editor at two newspapers and the Associated Press, Jacqueline Diamond enjoys researching medical issues and the world of private detectives for her books. She's written some ninety romances and mysteries, as well as teaching writing and raising two sons with Kurt, her husband of more than thirty years. The recipient of a career achievement award from *RT Book Reviews*, Jackie lives in Orange County, California, and invites you to visit her website, www.jacquelinediamond.com, for writing tips and the latest on her books. You're also welcome to email her at jdiamondfriends@yahoo.com to join her mailing list.

Books by Jacqueline Diamond

HARLEQUIN AMERICAN ROMANCE

To my friends and fellow writers at the
Orange County Chapter of Romance
Writers of America

Chapter One

It felt like a betrayal.

You're being irrational, Erica Benford told herself as her running shoes smacked a steady rhythm along the earthen track. *So what if all Dr. T talked about during surgery this morning were those*—she shuddered before mentally finishing the sentence—*those babies?*

Babies. Honestly.

People often assumed that Erica had chosen to work as a surgical nurse assisting one of the nation's leading fertility specialists because she loved babies. Well, she did, more or less, as long as they belonged to other women. And didn't intrude on the intelligent conversations that enlivened her hours in the operating room, conversations about everything from politics and scientific developments to the latest additions to the hospital staff.

Shrugging off her annoyance, she glanced past the civic center and nearby bluffs to the blue water shimmering far below in late-afternoon sunlight. The Pacific Ocean lapped serenely toward shore, while beyond a stretch of luxury homes, she glimpsed the welcoming curve of Safe Harbor, the marina from which this Southern California town took its name.

Less than a year after moving here, Erica still wasn't used to jogging outdoors on a February afternoon. Although she enjoyed the change from Boston's harsh winters, the weather hadn't figured into her decision to relocate. She'd leaped at the chance to escape the wreckage of a painful divorce and join Dr. T—as most people called Dr. Owen Tartikoff—who'd been hired to launch a major new fertility program at Safe Harbor Medical Center.

People referred to him as her "hospital husband," but Erica had never felt romantic about the perfectionist surgeon, whom she'd assisted in surgery for the past five years. She'd been worried at first when he fell in love with Bailey, one of the office nurses, but fortunately, his love life hadn't intruded on the O.R. Well, there had been some discussion when it turned out that Bailey was pregnant with twins, and everyone including Erica had happily attended the couple's wedding, but she'd assumed things would soon get back to normal.

She hadn't counted on the effect those babies would have on him. Did he have to yammer about them *all* during surgery today? What a strong grip the little boy had and how smart the little girl was, and on and on.

They were month-old infants, for Pete's sake. Tiny lumps with cute faces. Tiny lumps that required frequent feeding and diaper changes, as she recalled from the involuntary babysitting she'd done for her younger cousins long ago. All these years, she and Dr. T had shared the joke that, despite their profession, they took no interest in becoming parents. Her closest colleague, he'd understood her better than anyone.

No wonder she felt betrayed. It made her lungs ache just thinking about this morning's gooey account of precious baby Julie and oh-so-adorable Richard.

Don't forget to breathe, Erica reminded herself, and

sucked in a couple lungfuls of the crisp air as she rounded the far end of the track. That was when she noticed the man.

How long had this muscular fellow been pounding along behind her? There'd been a couple of high-school-age runners going through their paces when she'd arrived at the park a short while ago. When had they left?

The newcomer caught her look and responded with a slight nod. Erica ignored him. She just wished her gaze hadn't lingered a fraction of second longer than necessary, taking in the blue eyes, the thick, wavy hair that went from shades of dark brown to blond. Also, the fact that he limped and was pushing on in spite of it.

Okay, she'd also cataloged the way his shorts hugged his hips, and the appealing stretch of a Viva Arizona! T-shirt across his broad chest. Very nice build. And not too tall, either. At five foot two, Erica liked tall men, but not so tall they stumbled over her while dancing.

Oh, right. As if she was interested in picking up guys on the track, when she avoided gyms because she exercised for her health and peace of mind, not to troll for dates.

This guy apparently didn't register her scowl. He paced alongside—how irksome that he caught up easily, despite his limp—and matched his stride to hers.

In Boston, Erica would have greeted him with a classic "Beat it!" Or a simple, elegant "Get lost, buster." In California, however, she'd learned that opening remarks like that were considered rude. You had to wait until the guy said something obnoxious before you sent him packing.

"So which type of dumbbell are you escaping?" the man asked with a sideways grin.

She hadn't heard that line before. "Excuse me?"

"Sharp clothes, and you're in great shape, which means you're serious about exercising." His eyes swept her knowingly. "You'd enjoy the equipment at health clubs, so you must be avoiding them for a reason."

"Because I hate pickup artists." She ignored his slight wince. If his leg hurt, why didn't he knock off running? Or maybe he was reacting to her put-down.

Good. Leave me alone. Still, despite her bad mood, it was flattering to have an attractive man show an interest in her, considering the cutting remarks her husband had made when he'd dumped her. On top of that, after thirty years of enjoying male attention for her blond hair and trim figure, Erica didn't enjoy getting lost among Southern California's abundance of beauties.

Her response failed to dissuade her new jogging companion. "I'm not sure which I dislike most about gyms," he went on conversationally. "The camping queens who spread their water bottles, towels and backpacks all over the floor or the ones who yammer inanely on their cell phones."

"As if *women* were the problem!" Erica could give him a long list of men's failings, but started with "What about the weight lifters who grunt and make other disgusting noises? They're enough to make you swear off exercise."

"That's only one." His jaw twitched.

"One what?"

"One problem with guys. Compared to two for women."

Although she disliked talking while jogging, she couldn't let that remark pass. "No, it isn't. Pickup artists, remember?"

"You're saying women don't pick up men at health clubs?" He flexed his shoulders. Most likely that was a masculine move to emphasize their bulk, which she had to admit was rather impressive.

"Women might flirt, but they don't leer," she retorted.

"Besides, you can't tell me you don't belong to a health club. I can see you lift weights."

"You noticed? I'm honored." Big grin, as if he'd scored points. "I exercise at home."

"And in public parks."

"That, too." The man edged close enough for Erica to feel his body heat and inhale the appealing tang of aftershave lotion mixed with sweat.

She decided to try a different tack to put him off. "How'd you hurt your leg? Drop a dumbbell on it?"

He neither broke stride nor changed expression. "Somebody shot me."

Probably a woman you ran into on a track. It seemed churlish to say that, so she asked, "Why, exactly?"

"In the line of duty."

On this stretch, they faced the police department, which occupied a two-story stucco building in the civic center. Well, that explained a lot. "You're a cop?"

"Detective," he said. "My name's Lock, short for Sherlock. Guess I didn't have much choice about my profession."

"Your parents named you after Sherlock Holmes?" Erica wasn't sure whether or not to believe a word he said. In her experience men lied about almost anything, including their names, to impress women.

"Less a tribute to his detective skills than to his drug use, I suspect."

"That's cynical."

"You never met my parents. Lucky you." A note of bitterness crept into his voice, and he eased away.

Erica felt an unwilling flash of sympathy. If you could believe him, the guy had overcome a troubled background, dedicated himself to serving the public and been shot for his efforts. "Were you badly injured?"

"I gained some interesting metallic parts that add to the fun of going through airport security," Lock said. "By the way, it's customary when a man tells you his name to respond with yours."

"Is that what you teach women about personal security, Officer?"

He ducked his head. "Touché."

That was a sweet response. Why was she being so prickly with him, anyway? "Erica," she said.

"It suits you. Starts and ends with a soft vowel but that hard *C* adds bite," he said. "Speaking of bites, you hungry?"

They'd just met and he was asking her to dinner? Still, must be near five, and growing dark. "What did you have in mind?"

"I'm a good cook."

Now that *was* nervy, expecting her to accompany him home. "I'm sure we could find someplace near here to eat. Not that Safe Harbor has the world's best supply of restaurants."

"Oh, you discovered that already?"

Something about his question troubled her. "What do you mean, 'already'?"

Lock took a moment to answer. Not a very long moment, but up till now he'd had a rapid-fire response to everything. "You're not from around here."

"What makes you say that?"

"Your accent."

True, she did tend to use broad *A* sounds and swallow the letter *R,* but tired of being teased by coworkers about *pahk*ing her *cah* in *Hahvahd yahd,* she'd been working on her Boston pronunciation. Anyway, that wasn't the point. Some people lived in a place for years without losing their old accent. "Have you been spying on me, Detective?"

Maybe she was paranoid, but after her ex-husband's

cheating and lying, she tended to think the worst of guys. In the weeks since she'd started jogging here, she hadn't noticed Lock before, but the police department was right next door. He might have seen her walk to her sedan, then scoped out her license plate. Also, the windshield still bore a parking sticker from her old hospital back East, right next to the new one. That was all she needed, another manipulative male.

Again, Lock paused for a second too long. "I'm not a stalker. Look, I'm sorry if we got off on the wrong foot…"

Erica halted in middle of the track. "As far as I'm concerned, Detective, you have two wrong feet. Frankly, I find you a little creepy."

His head jerked as if she'd slapped him. "I'm nothing like that. Which you'd realize if you got to know me better."

"I'll have to take your word for that, because I have no intention of dining with you. Tonight or any other night."

Without giving him a chance to reply, she cut away from the track. It galled Erica to see the flash of hurt in his eyes. As her feet carried her toward the parking lot, she had to force herself not to glance back.

But she knew her weakness for men who combined a rough exterior with an air of vulnerability. She'd learned the hard way that you could never tame a guy like that. You just ended up being played for a fool.

Still, as she slid behind the wheel, she allowed herself one final peek toward the track. There was no sign of Detective Sherlock.

Erica put the car in gear and headed toward her apartment a few blocks away. She'd be back, though. No man was going to drive her away from her favorite park. If he bothered her again, she'd report him for harassment.

Well, maybe, said a traitorous voice inside.

CREEPY? LOCK VAUGHN had never been called that before.

Irked, he whipped his gunmetal-gray coupe to a halt at one side of the small shopping center lot, leaving more convenient spaces for clients. Not that many customers showed up in person at Fact Hunter Investigations.

In the case he'd almost completed, the client, Ginnifer Moran, lived on the opposite side of the country. Despite the distance, the well-to-do businesswoman had decided to check out the stories her fiancé told about his ex-wife. If Erica Benford was an out-of-control alcoholic who picked up strangers for sex, her husband had been justified in leaving her.

If not, he was a liar and a gold digger.

None of the stories had proved true, Lock reflected as he limped toward the investigation company's door, wedged between an escrow company and the Sexy Over Sixty Gym. In Erica's trash, he'd found a single wine bottle, plus a supermarket receipt that listed a six-pack of beer. No sign of drugs or contraceptives, either. A records check had shown excellent credit and a clean driving record, while discreet inquiries had turned up a spotless reputation at the hospital. As he could testify from observation, she didn't hang out at bars and she kept regular hours. The agency Ginnifer had hired in Boston had come up empty-handed, as well.

Erica's only sins appeared to be an overreliance on take-out food and a rush to judgment on men. But given a lying ex-husband intent on blackening her name, she had good reason to be suspicious.

Also, she'd been right. Lock did have an ulterior motive.

Still, *creepy?* The word rankled. He might not be the world's smoothest operator, but he'd never had a problem interesting ladies when he put forth the effort.

He opened the door stenciled with the agency's name and paused to rub his sore thigh before tackling the flight of stairs to the second-floor office. If he worked for someone else, he'd have insisted on an elevator. Being coowner meant he appreciated the modest rent and considered this climb part of his rehab. On a bad day, he could use the service elevator, but the way it creaked and jerked hurt his leg just as much, without the benefit of exercise.

Last spring, after he and his foster brother, Mike Aaron, bought this agency in their native Southern California, Lock had handed in his two-week notice at the sheriff's department in Flagstaff, Arizona. The next day, while off duty, he'd stumbled across a bank holdup. The robber's aim hadn't been as good as Lock's, but it had done enough damage to lay him up for months. He regretted not being able to arrive sooner to join Mike, whose friendship had helped him stay straight during his difficult teen years.

Slowly, Lock stumped up the steps. Despite the pain, it had felt good to stretch out on a track. He just wished he hadn't been there to fulfill a final demand by the client. Left to his own conscience, Lock would have refused to try to pick up Erica Benford, even though, had she fallen for it, he'd have faked an emergency phone call rather than take her home. He wasn't sure what accepting his invitation would have proved, anyway. Agreeing to let him cook dinner was a far cry from leaping into bed. And even if she had, so what? Nobody these days expected a single woman to live like a hermit.

But the client was willing to pay well for the firm's services, and as Mike pointed out, owning a business didn't come cheap. So Lock had given it his best shot.

And offended a very attractive lady.

At the top of the stairs, he went through a windowed door marked with the firm's name and paused to enjoy the sight of the freshly painted and carpeted outer office. Framed certificates, awards and commendations from his deputy sheriff's position and Mike's work at the Safe Harbor Police Department lined one wall. Across from them, a trio of paintings in splashes of amber, coral and aqua depicted the Grand Canyon—eighty miles from Flagstaff—at different times of day. Lock had bought them at an outdoor art sale and shipped them here.

At the reception desk, Sue Carrera, the middle-aged secretary who doubled as bookkeeper, whisked a tissue from the box in front of her. "Ready to have lipstick scrubbed off?"

"No lipstick." In such a small office, everyone knew your business.

She set down the tissue box. "Silly me. She wouldn't put on lipstick to go jogging."

"That isn't why—"

A stocky young woman with short, straight, blond hair popped her head out of the report-writing room. "Did she take the bait?"

Why did everyone have such a keen interest in this assignment? "No." Lock braced himself for a raucous comment about striking out. That would be typical male commentary, and Detective Patty Denny, while unmistakably female, had an ex-cop's reputation as one of the guys.

Instead, she gave a satisfied nod. "Good. I was rooting for Erica."

"Why's that?"

"Alec likes her, remember?"

"Oh, right."

Patty's new husband, an embryologist who was part of the medical team that had relocated from Boston to California, had a long acquaintance with Erica. Patty had solicited his opinion without revealing that they were investigating his colleague, and reported that he considered Erica an outstanding scrub nurse and all-around good person. Lock had also questioned a male nurse who, he'd learned from Patty, was a notorious gossip, and the fellow hadn't said anything worse than that Erica seemed stand-offish.

The door to Mike's office opened to reveal a lanky, sandy-haired man wearing a pair of reading glasses he'd acquired in the past few months. A result of all the paperwork, he'd complained only half in jest. "Batting zero again, eh, bro?" he asked, no doubt having overheard the conversation.

"What do you mean, again?" Lock raised an eyebrow. "I seem to recall drawing this mission because of certain studly qualities that might—and I do mean this in the nicest way—be otherwise lacking around here."

"That's kind of tough on Patty, don't you think?" Mike peered down from his six-foot-four-inch height. "Ms. Benford turned you down flat?"

"Flat as a tortilla."

Mike shrugged. "Guess that's a wrap, then."

"Ouch," said Patty.

Both men regarded her questioningly.

"Bad pun," she told them. "Tortilla—wrap. Wrapping up the case. That reminds me, I'm hungry. Got to pick up groceries on the way home." Although her dining preferences ran to pizza and chocolate bars, Patty took her new role as stepmother to a five-year-old girl seriously.

"Isn't it your husband's turn to shop?" Mike had a weird habit of keeping track of all sorts of things.

"Yeah, but he tends to go out at lunch and store the food in a refrigerator at work. He swears he doesn't keep it near those embryos, but I'm not taking any chances."

Mike grimaced. "I don't blame you."

Lock checked his watch. Nearly five. He'd like to write up this afternoon's incident while it was fresh in his mind. Every detail mattered, because you never knew when a case might end up in court, where attorneys picked things apart under a mental microscope. "Have fun at the supermarket. See you later."

The desk in his private office, next to Mike's, was bare except for a few manila folders and a copy of California's Private Investigator Act, which Lock was studying to prepare for his licensing exam. That left plenty of room to open his laptop and take out the voice recorder into which he'd described the encounter while driving.

From below came the faint creak of exercise equipment, or maybe that was the creak of elderly joints being put through a workout. Lock didn't mind the muted noise. At the house he and Mike shared, his brother spent at least an hour a day on a treadmill that sounded as if it hadn't been oiled since the late Jurassic.

Both brothers disdained gyms, with their complicated machines, body odors and rude patrons who failed to rerack their weights and wipe them clean of their sweat. Lock hadn't been kidding in his remarks to Erica, but he doubted anything would convince her of that.

As he transcribed and added to his notes, an image intruded on his thoughts: of Erica's small figure filling out the pink jogging suit. As he'd approached from behind, he'd noted the luscious shape of her derriere and the tantalizing blond hair that bounced across her shoulders. Then, when he came alongside, her fierce hazel eyes had swept him sharply enough to knock a lesser man off his stride.

Lock couldn't explain the jolt that had gone through him. Chemistry, sure, but something more complicated, too. A sense that he knew her. Not surprising, considering that he'd been investigating her for weeks. But also, he'd had the strange impression when he met her eyes that he'd caught a glimpse of his own soul.

Now what the hell was that about?

His training had kicked in, and he'd sprung his opening line on her smoothly enough. But he longed to find out what his reaction meant, even though he knew better than to get involved with a woman whose trash he'd rifled through, and whom he was even now writing up in cold, analytical terms. She'd never forgive him if she learned the truth, and he had an ethical obligation to keep his private life separate from his professional work.

Yet…what was it about Erica Benford that vibrated inside him on a wavelength he'd never shared with anyone? Maybe if he figured out the secret of that connection, he'd finally understand why he'd really come back to California.

Chapter Two

The next day, a storm rolled in. Although the weather forecasters assured the public it had arrived across the warm Pacific rather than descending from chilly Alaska, the temperature dropped and more than an inch of rain turned the dry earth to mud. Much as Erica longed to go jogging, she stuck to the hospital's exercise room when it wasn't being used for childbirth classes.

Although the rain stopped after a few days, it left a soggy landscape that kept her confined. By Friday, she felt ready to claw open the nearest hospital window and dive into a bedraggled bed of petunias. But she couldn't really blame the weather for her troubled mood.

Friday marked the tenth anniversary of the worst day of Erica's life. It was also her birthday, which meant someone might—if she was unlucky—expect her to celebrate. If so, she'd have to plaster a fake smile on her face, because the last thing she wanted to share with anyone was that not only had her world been shattered the day she turned twenty-one, but she sometimes felt as if she'd stuck the pieces together with glue that might crumble at any moment.

Mercifully, a full schedule in the operating room kept her focused. Dr. Owen Tartikoff loved performing surgery, and Erica felt the joy radiating from his broad smile to the roots of his russet hair. The source was partly the challenge and reward of restoring women's fertility, but also the sheer fun of working with the hospital's state-of-the-art equipment.

While the use of thin scopes fitted with cameras had become routine in surgery, doctors at Safe Harbor now had access to a million-dollar system called a da Vinci robot. For complex procedures, Dr. T would sit at the console's controls, viewing the surgical site through a high-resolution endoscopic camera, and maneuver several robotic arms with jointed wrists that were able to refine the surgery to a precision even the most skilled hands couldn't produce.

"Coolest tools in the world," the obstetrician remarked gleefully as he performed a myomectomy to remove uterine fibroids from a thirty-five-year-old patient who'd been trying to get pregnant for years.

Erica handed a sterile instrument to Dr. Zack Sargent, who was assisting. He followed Dr. T's instructions to retract some patient tissue. "So, do we have a date yet for Ms. Garcia's arrival?" Zack asked.

"You just can't wait to get that egg-donor program started, can you?" remarked anesthesiologist Rod Vintner from the specialized computer terminal where he monitored the patient's vital signs.

"Some of us enjoy helping women have babies," Zack said drily.

"Seems to be a lot of that going around." Rod was as cynical about babies as Erica.

"I'm afraid everything's on hold until September," Dr. T said. "Jan's current hospital is invoking some contractual right or other." He'd jumped at the chance to hire nurse administrator Jan Garcia to coordinate the planned egg-donor program at Safe Harbor. It was a program that particularly interested Zack, an earnest young ob-gyn.

Erica was disappointed about the delay, too, although not because of any interest in the new project. She liked Jan, with whom she'd worked in Boston before Jan took the Houston job three years ago. It would be nice to see her again and to have a female friend here in California.

"That's a bummer," Zack said. "As you've pointed out, the staff's having a postholiday letdown. And our publicity's dropped off since the grand opening."

"The press has a short memory," Owen observed. "That can be a curse or a blessing."

Last September had marked the official launch of the fertility program. Thanks in part to Dr. T's fame and a new procedure he'd pioneered, the event had drawn widespread interest from the media. There'd also been unwelcome coverage of his half brother's indictment in a fraud scheme, for which the man was now serving a long sentence.

Personally, Erica could do without seeing the hospital's name splashed across the news. Still, a for-profit facility depended on attracting new patients, and while the public relations director did her best, she couldn't singlehandedly keep Safe Harbor Medical in the public eye.

"I'm open to ideas," Dr. T said from his console. "As long as they don't involve a reality TV show. The only camera I want to see around here is that one." He indicated the overhead device that recorded each operation for later review. It also allowed them to televise surgeries to medical schools and other hospitals for teaching purposes, although they weren't doing that today.

"We could operate in our underwear," Rod said sardonically. "That oughta make the ten o'clock news."

"For all the wrong reasons," Zack replied, without removing his gaze from the patient.

The anesthesiologist shrugged. "What can I say? Sex sells."

"You in your underwear?" Dr. T said. "That's a stretch."

"I'm a sexy guy. Ask anyone." Rod jerked his thumb toward Zack. "Except him."

Erica pretended to be absorbed in examining the instrument tray. She hoped no one noticed the heat spreading across her cheeks because of the picture that sprang to mind at the mention of sexy guys. One of thick, brown-blond hair, a T-shirt clinging to a broad chest, shorts hugging narrow hips... Much as she longed to, she couldn't keep the images of the breezily confident Lock out of her thoughts.

She wasn't likely see him again. Certainly not until the park dried out enough for her to resume jogging.

"I'd welcome an idea that'll build staff morale and interest the press, not reduce us all to helpless laughter," said Dr. T.

"A baby photo contest?" Zack suggested.

"That's lame." Catching the ob-gyn's irritated glance, the anesthesiologist assumed an innocent expression. "Just expressing an opinion."

"What about another kind of contest? Something concerning the fertility rate," Erica volunteered. "But not multiple births, of course." That would be medically inappropriate, since such births, while of interest to the public, could endanger the health of moms and babies.

Owen nodded approvingly, sending a warm glow through Erica. "You're on the right track. That bears thinking about."

"Thanks."

Dr. T gave further instructions to Zack, and for a while they were all absorbed in wrapping up the operation. Only when he'd moved away from the console did Owen address her again, and then merely to ask if she planned to have lunch in the cafeteria.

Erica checked the clock. It was nearly three-thirty and she'd been on duty since seven that morning. While she ate snacks to keep up her energy level, she hadn't consumed anything substantial during her half hour lunch break. "Guess so."

"I might see you there," was all he said.

Now what did that mean? As she stripped off her scrubs, Erica reflected uneasily that the doctor was aware of her birthday. While Owen wasn't the type who lavished his staff with gifts, he could surprise you when you least expected it.

Or wanted it.

Deciding to avoid him by grabbing a sandwich from a vending machine, she strolled to the second-floor break room. There, she found the machine empty of everything except gooey bear claws and salty peanuts, the same stuff she'd been snacking on earlier.

Her stomach rebelled. Erica supposed she'd better listen to the warning.

She took the stairs down a flight. On the main floor, she caught a whiff of Friday's special, poached fish, and speeded her pace toward the cafeteria.

A glance showed more tables occupied than usual for this hour, probably because the cool temperatures kept people from spreading out onto the patio. Erica took a tray and approached the hot-food serving line, only to find it closed.

"Sorry," said the cashier from her central register. "All we've got left are sandwiches."

Glumly, Erica turned to the depleted array of foods and picked a small fruit plate and a glass of milk. In Boston, she would have joined friends, but she hadn't formed any close ties since arriving in Safe Harbor. With new acquaintances, conversations tended to turn to personal matters such as marital status, which was still a sore subject. At her old hospital, she hadn't had to explain anything, because everyone had watched the melodrama unfold in real time.

She'd met Donald Panzer while volunteering at the substance abuse clinic where he worked. A former addict, he'd earned a master's degree in social work and now counseled others. Energetic and personable, he'd showered Erica with attention when she felt vulnerable, appealed to her nurturing side when she caught him in lies, and cheated on her repeatedly. By the time she faced the fact that her two-year marriage was a sham, he'd taken up with a wealthy business owner named Ginnifer Moran and set his sights on marrying her. Even though he'd readily agreed to divorce, he'd spread ugly rumors about Erica, as if trying to justify himself. She'd been glad to reclaim her maiden name of Benford and put that whole mess behind her.

Now, she looked around for an empty table, until she noticed someone waving at her. It was Ned Norwalk, the blond, surfer-type nurse who assisted Owen in his office and with whom Erica sometimes had to coordinate scheduling. Sitting beside him was one of the hospital volunteers, an older woman with graying, light brown hair framing a strong face.

"I'm surprised to see you here during office hours," Erica told Ned as she set down her tray. "Don't you have patients?" Although Owen didn't schedule regular appointments on Friday afternoons, he used the time for follow-ups and urgent referrals.

"It's slower than usual." That still didn't account for Ned choosing to buy coffee in the cafeteria when he kept a pot brewing in the office.

"No wonder it's slow. Southern Californians hunker down when the temperature drops below seventy," said his companion with a cheerful lilt. "My name's Renée Green, by the way."

"Glad to meet you. I'm Erica."

"Oh, I know who you are." She smiled. "Bailey talks about you a lot."

"How do you know Bailey?" Dr. T's wife had gone on maternity leave from her nursing job months ago.

"We met through a community counseling center," Renée said. "If it weren't for her, I'd never have thought of volunteering here, and I love it. This hospital feels like my second home."

That makes two of us, Erica reflected as she finished a bite of cantaloupe. "You don't work?" She waved a hand apologetically. "I don't mean to sound dismissive. I just wondered…"

"Why I'm free in the middle of the afternoon? I recently retired from my job as a receptionist at an insurance company," the woman explained. "I'm a widow, so my time is my own. How about you?"

Uh-oh. It was a familiar pattern: *I'll tell you my story and now you tell me yours.*

Erica was spared having to deflect the question because Renée was no longer watching her. The woman's face lit up as she gazed toward the cafeteria entrance. "Look who's here! Aren't they adorable?"

"They almost make *me* want to have kids," Ned agreed. For once, Erica didn't mind when she spotted the twins in their double stroller. She was more than willing to let them monopolize this conversation.

Besides, they were awfully cute. The little boy had bright red hair that would likely darken to match his father's, while Julie, who was wriggling around in her seat, had curly brown hair with a hint of red, like her mother's. Behind the stroller, Bailey beamed with pride. Her handsome husband radiated high spirits as he followed her into view carrying a sheet cake blazing with candles.

Erica barely stifled a groan.

"Happy birthday!" cried Ned and Renée.

They'd come here because of her? So, apparently, had many of the other cafeteria visitors, who burst into a chorus of "Happy Birthday," led by Dr. T's baritone.

A lump formed in Erica's throat as she took in the genial faces of her colleagues. Along with several fellow nurses, she spotted nursing director Betsy Raditch, hospital administrator Dr. Mark Rayburn, embryologist Alec Denny and public relations director Jennifer Serra Martin. They'd all gathered to wish her well.

And none of them had the slightest idea how very unwell this day made her feel.

Erica forced a pleasant expression onto her face. "Thank you, everybody," she said when the singing stopped. "This is a treat."

"It's spice cake—your favorite. I have that on good authority," Bailey said as her husband set down the cake. "I'm going to let the surgeon do the cutting. He's better at it than I am."

Owen flexed his hands. "Anybody want a slice?"

They all did. The cake was delicious, and to Erica's amazement, some of her coworkers had brought her presents. Owen and Bailey gave her a generous gift certificate to A Memorable Décor, her favorite local store, which specialized in antique-style furnishings. Alec presented her with a couple of velvet cushions in shades of pink, hand-embroidered with butterflies, from him and his wife, Patty. It surprised her that he remembered how much she liked butterflies.

"You shop at A Memorable Décor?" Renée's eyes sparkled. "I love that place!"

"Yes, although they're a little pricey," Erica admitted. "Mostly I haunt thrift shops. But I'll enjoy spending this."

"I'm sorry I didn't bring you a gift," Renée said.

"Don't be silly. I'm amazed that anyone went to all this trouble," she assured her.

Soon the gathering broke up. Unlike Erica, most of the attendees still had an hour or so left in their workday. She went out alone, carrying the cushions in their pretty shopping bag and balancing the leftover cake in a catering box. Along the walkway that led to the parking garage, rays of late-afternoon sunshine brought out the vibrant purples and yellows in a bed of pansies. It hadn't been such a bad birthday, after all.

The screech of brakes and the furious blare of a horn sent her heart thundering into her throat. A short distance away, a laundry service van had pulled out in front of a flower delivery truck, which missed it by inches. The drivers glared at each other and then the van backed out of the way.

Erica felt her heart pumping hard as she headed to her car. She was shaking so badly she could barely balance the cake on the bumper as she opened the trunk to put everything inside.

The near collision had banished her sense of well-being, leaving a void quickly filled by a rush of guilt. *How could I laugh and enjoy myself, today of all days?*

She sat behind the wheel until she stopped trembling. She needed to shake this off and restore her equilibrium.

She'd unload her stuff at home, change clothes and drive to the park. If the track was still muddy, she could run on the grass until she was too tired to do anything but collapse in front of the TV and stuff herself with spice cake.

LOCK HADN'T BEEN thinking about Erica the entire week, just most of it. Hard not to, while he wrote up the results of the investigation, complete with photos. Even the shots taken in less-than-ideal light and from quirky angles showed those soulful eyes and her generous mouth.

He hadn't concentrated on her case exclusively, of course. He'd conducted background checks on a couple of new employees for a large company, testified in a custody case about the husband's motel dates with female companions and located a missing autistic man at a video arcade. He'd also checked the park a few times, but in view of the rainy weather, wasn't surprised that Erica stayed away.

Give it up, Lock told himself on Friday afternoon. Having worked the previous evening, he felt justified in knocking off early, but he did *not* feel justified in trying to contact a woman he'd checked out for a client.

Yet he steered automatically toward City Hall Park. The thing was, Lock reflected, he ought to have one more casual conversation with Erica so he could get past this inexplicable sense that they were connected.

As he pulled into the nearly empty lot, a small dog ran in front of his car. Lock hit the brakes and was glad when the pooch fled unharmed.

Since dogs weren't allowed to run loose in Safe Harbor, this fluffy critter must be someone's lost pet. After parking, Lock surveyed the area. No sign of Fluffy. He circled along a walkway, whistling and calling, "Here, boy!" For good measure, he tried, "Here, girl!" Neither produced any results. Except for a few hardy skateboarders trying tricks farther along on the cement path, the park appeared deserted.

Lock made one more swing around the parking lot. In a corner, he spotted a familiar blue sedan with hospital decals on the windshield. A surge of pleasure lifted his spirits. She'd come back.

He parked and set out for the track. Topping a slight rise, he was disappointed not to spot Erica's slim figure anywhere on the beaten oval. Even from here, he could see lingering puddles that indicated it was too muddy for running. Where had she gone?

The swish of running shoes made him turn. "Well, well, if it isn't Sherlock Holmes," said the keen-eyed blonde with what might have been either a smile or a grimace. Hard to tell which as she raced past on the grass. "Looking for clues, Detective?"

Although he hadn't dressed for exercise, Lock pushed off, enjoying the view of the dark rose track suit stretching over her lithe figure. He ignored the twinges in his leg as he lengthened his stride to catch her. "I'd like to explain something. About my being a detective…"

Her gaze bathed him in skepticism. "Don't tell me. You made that up."

"No, but I did give you the wrong impression. I don't work for the police department," he said as they crunched across a scattering of fallen twigs.

"Who do you work for?"

"Private agency." He caught a whiff of jasmine. Perfume, shampoo or a nearby flowering bush? Didn't matter. The scent seemed to float around Erica.

"Confession is good for the soul," she returned, "but why bother?"

"Because I like you."

She came to a stop, hands on hips, chest swelling as she caught her breath. Wisps of blond hair haloed her face. "First impressions aside, I'm willing to grant that you're a nice enough guy, Sherlock, or whatever your real name is."

"Lock Vaughn," he said. "And there's a 'but' coming, isn't there? How about if we discuss it over dinner?"

"No, thanks. You've picked a bad day to try to charm me or whatever you're doing," Erica said.

"I don't want anything more than friendship. Of an extremely casual nature," Lock assured her. At the moment, he meant it.

"It always starts that way."

"Believe me—"

"That's the thing, Detective. I'm not big on believing people. And like I said, you have terrible timing."

Usually, Lock was able to keep a step ahead of the women he met, which helped in winning them over. But Erica thought as fast as he did, and now she caught him off guard by swiveling and racing away. Despite the urge to go after her, better judgment prevailed. The lady had said no.

From the rise, Lock watched her angle down toward the sidewalk that edged Civic Center Drive. Then loud barking drew his attention away—to Fluffy, racing on short legs across the ground, with a big, scraggly dog loping behind him.

Lock saw Erica glance toward the barking and stop, as if trying to decide what to do. The larger dog eased off, but Fluffy, too terrified to notice, leaped into the street with a frightened yelp.

From his vantage point, Lock registered the approach of a fast-moving sport utility vehicle. With a jolt, he flashed on what was about to happen.

Furiously, he pelted across the grass, yelling, "Look out!" Erica frowned in his direction, unable to see what was so clear to him.

Just as he'd known would happen, brakes squealed and the SUV swerved to avoid the panic-stricken little dog. The vehicle leaped the low curb and skidded out of control.

Straight toward Erica.

Chapter Three

She'd almost felt guilty for abandoning Lock when he'd been trying so hard to ingratiate himself. The guy was an intriguing mix of rough edges and smooth talk that Erica couldn't quite figure out, and once upon a time she'd have stuck around to explore what lay beneath the surface.

But despite the instincts drawing her toward him, she'd had to break away. Had to run until her brain shut down and she forgot everything except straining muscles and the thrum of her heart.

A burst of barking had drawn her attention to a couple of dogs. As she'd weighed whether to risk intervening, the bigger dog gave up the chase. Now why had that little pooch kept on running, right into the street? She'd heard Lock shout, but that was only likely to frighten the dog further.

Then she saw the detective waving at her in alarm. At the same moment, a crunch of tires drew Erica's attention to the SUV veering toward her, a woman gripping the steering wheel in obvious panic. Although it appeared she had time to stop, she hit the accelerator by mistake, making the vehicle leap forward.

Erica's legs grew leaden, as if gravity had tripled its hold. Which way to go? Either direction might put her in the path of this unpredictable driver.

The daylight dimmed. Erica heard the shriek of metal and the sickening crunch of glass, and felt a heavy body slamming into her. Someone was lifting her, falling on her—no, that had been years ago, a decade ago—yanking her up the hill, and the car swerved again, jounced back onto the pavement and jolted to a halt.

Tremors racked Erica so hard she feared her knees would fold. Strong arms wrapped around her, gathering her against a solid male chest.

Vaguely, she heard a woman crying, "Are you all right? I'm so sorry. I was trying to miss that dog."

"You nearly hit her." The outrage in Lock's voice rumbled through Erica.

"Is she injured? I have insurance." The woman came into focus, fidgeting on the sidewalk. She appeared to be in her forties, and wearing a tailored pantsuit and high heels as she was, had probably just left work. "I'm driving my husband's SUV because my car's in the shop, and I'm not used to it. Should I call an ambulance?"

"No." Erica didn't need paramedics. She just wanted to go home.

The woman rummaged in her purse and pulled out a wallet. "Here's my driver's license and insurance card. You should write this down. You might discover later that you've twisted something. I guess we should call the police, too, shouldn't we?"

"That's up to Erica. There was no collision." Lock sounded reassuringly calm, although she could still hear the anger in his voice.

Erica shivered. She couldn't face the police with their endless questions and delays. Besides, what was there to say? "I'm okay."

"All the same, we should take her information." Releasing her, Lock copied the data from the documents into a small notebook.

"Call me if you have any problem, anything at all." The woman's voice cracked, and Erica realized the incident had shaken her, too.

"I do have a request." Lock pointed across the street, where the small dog was sniffing around a covered trash can. Its former pursuer had vanished. "See if you can find that dog's owner. There's a tag on his collar."

"Of course!" She sounded relieved at having something to do.

"And get your tires checked. You may have damaged them with that maneuver," he added.

"I will. Thank you! And again, I'm so sorry." Off went the woman. Erica was pleased to see her carefully approach the little dog, which backed off a few steps but wagged its tail and let her pick it up.

"Happy ending," said Lock.

"Let's hope." As her fear eased, it occurred to Erica that she was acting like a scared stray herself. "Thanks for shoring me up. I don't know what came over me."

"Shock. It's a natural reaction." Up close, she could see the rough grain of his skin and the inviting curve of his mouth.

"Well, I'm over it."

"Don't count on that. Traffic accidents can traumatize people even when they're physically unharmed."

"I thought you weren't a cop," Erica retorted, taking refuge in irony.

Lock studied her sympathetically. "Until recently, I was a sheriff's deputy in Coconino County, Arizona."

"And now, by sheer luck, you find yourself in California, rescuing women in pink jogging suits?" she responded, trying to ignore the cold bite of the breeze.

Around them, the shadows had lengthened as the early February darkness closed in.

He reached for her hands. "Let's get you to a warm place."

"I'm fine."

"You're trembling."

Erica hadn't noticed, but he was right. "Walk me to my car. I'll turn the heater up full blast, I promise."

"Glad to."

With Lock keeping pace, she ignored the traitorous liquidity of her knees and made her way across the grass. It took all her focus to maintain her balance on the uneven ground.

"The blood's drained out of your face," Lock said when they reached the pavement. "Trust me, shock is nothing to take lightly."

As a nurse, Erica knew he was right—and wrong. "This isn't shock. I haven't suffered an injury or blood loss, and my organs are in no danger of failing. It's a reaction to a surge of adrenaline, and I suppose an emotional response, as well."

Lock quirked an eyebrow. "Don't have a lot of respect for emotional responses, do you?"

"Do *you?*" she retorted, and dug into her pocket for her keys.

He blinked, which she was learning indicated she'd struck a nerve. "I'm a guy."

"Feelings aren't important to men?"

"I keep a tight lid on them. I'm not saying that's healthy, just that it's normal." He leaned against her car.

"As compared to women, who get the vapors and swoon into the nearest pair of male arms?" Pointless or not, the argument helped restore her sense of control.

"I'm game to do it again if you are." The man had a heart-stopping smile. She had to tear her gaze away.

There was only one other vehicle in the lot, a gray coupe with the lines of a sports car, Erica saw as she open the locks with a beep. Somehow she'd expected him to drive a jacked-up pickup. But as a detective, he was wise to keep his wheels inconspicuous. "I've done all the swooning I care to for one day. Have a nice evening, Detective."

"I should follow you home."

Great gimmick, Erica mused as she got into her car. Then he'd know where she lived, if he hadn't figured that out already. "No, thanks."

He stepped back. Erica angled the key toward the ignition. To her annoyance, it took three tries to insert it. *Keep your brain on track.*

She sat holding the steering wheel and willing herself to turn on the engine. Put the car in gear and drive to her apartment.

Her limbs refused to obey.

Lock tapped on the window. Erica wanted to ignore him, but common sense prevailed. Grimly, she pulled out the key, retrieved her purse and opened the door. "I guess I do need a ride."

"I'll pick you up tomorrow morning and bring you back here."

"I can call a cab." She was being ungracious, Erica knew, so she added, "Thank you for the offer. I'm not usually like this."

"I didn't expect you were."

They crossed the lot to his coupe. He held her elbow, steadying her. "Ever been in a bad accident?" he asked. "What's happening with you seems like a flashback."

"Yes." Might as well tell him. "Ten years ago, my brother was killed."

"I'm sorry." When she was safely inside, he closed the door and came around.

The car's scent suited him, Erica thought, inhaling a trace of leather and a hint of coffee from a take-out cup sitting in a holder. The lines were sporty, with the latest high-tech devices in the dash.

Nothing like Jordan's old car when he'd rattled to the curb in front of her nursing school ten years ago, grinning in a slightly loopy way as he peered out the window. "Hey, you think I'd let my kid sister ride the subway on her twenty-first birthday?" he'd called.

Erica had had to move classified ads and a number of job applications off the passenger seat before she sat down. On the floor, a take-out sack had rustled and released the odor of stale French fries. There'd been another scent in the air, too, the scent of marijuana. But she hadn't noticed that until after her brother gunned the engine and jerked into traffic, nearly clipping the shuttle bus she usually rode....

"What's going on?" Lock's voice brought her back to the present. They were rolling past the library.

"Remembering things I'd rather forget," Erica said. "Do you need directions to my apartment or do you already know where it is?"

Again, that telltale blink. "I could use directions."

She leaned back in the seat. "Go straight."

"Okay. Hungry?" he asked.

"It is dinnertime." Erica hoped he couldn't hear the rumblings from her stomach. The fruit plate, even finished off with a slice of cake, hadn't lasted long.

Lock paused at a stop sign. "Left, right or straight up?"

"This car flies?"

"I keep hoping, with all these gadgets."

"Left." Erica had another question. "Do you carry a gun?" She'd seen enough gunshot wounds to be leery of weapons.

He eased left. "Not since I handed in my badge. Now that you know what a harmless creature I am, I assume you'll let me cook dinner."

"Pushy." Erica had to laugh. She was feeling more comfortable, and for once she had no desire to return to an empty apartment. "I don't have much food on hand. Enough to rustle up something, I guess."

"Done." Lock turned into her complex. Apparently he didn't need any further directions.

Erica decided not to worry about that.

SURVIVING AN ACCIDENT that killed her brother couldn't help but leave a lasting psychic wound. No wonder Erica had reacted so strongly to the near miss with the SUV.

As he escorted her up the exterior staircase to her apartment, Lock didn't miss the shakiness in her movements. He admired her determined effort to ignore it.

On the upper walkway, waiting as Erica pulled out her key, he supposed he'd overstepped by insisting on making dinner for her. How would he explain this if Mike found out?

Still, Lock couldn't leave until he was certain she'd recovered enough to manage on her own. A hot meal ought to help. He owed her that much for invading her privacy in the first place. And he wanted the satisfaction of knowing she no longer ranked him as a creep.

As for his earlier impression that they had connected on some spiritual level, in retrospect it seemed misguided. They might share a cynical attitude about relationships with the opposite sex, but as the door opened on a cozy apartment stuffed with cushy furniture, Tiffany-style lamps and framed photographs of butterflies, Lock had to admit the resemblance didn't extend to decorating choices. The only thing he'd stuck on his bedroom wall was a dartboard, and if the house he and Mike rented hadn't come furnished, he'd be sleeping on an inflatable mattress.

"Nice stuff," he said, following her inside. She'd made the most of the modest living room, tucking a round table into one corner and filling part of a wall with an antique-style mirror that made the place look bigger.

"I'm the queen of thrift store shopping," Erica informed him as she untied her shoes. Lock set his next to hers on a small mat and tossed his jacket over the back of a chair.

On the counter that divided the living room from the compact kitchen, he caught sight of a cake box. "By the way, happy birthday."

She regarded him suspiciously. "How did you know it's my birthday?"

Oops. "I just assumed that was a birthday cake." But with the lid shut, there was no way he could have known.

"Don't lie to me. I hate that." Erica folded her arms. The movement pushed her breasts into prominence, as if Lock hadn't been keenly aware of them already. "You've been snooping."

No sense hiding a fact that was sure to surface sooner or later. "I work with someone you know. Patty Denny."

She took a moment to place the name. "Oh. Alec's wife. Why didn't you say so?"

"I'm in the habit of keeping things to myself." When this explanation failed to soften her expression, he added, "You can ask Patty all about me, if you're curious." Still, Lock hoped she wouldn't, because that was likely to lead to Mike finding out that he'd visited Erica's apartment.

He should leave. And would, as soon as they ate.

In the kitchen, Erica opened a cabinet. "I've got pasta and tomato sauce. Or we could send out for pizza."

"It's your birthday. You deserve a home-cooked meal." Lock nearly added, *"And you eat way too much fast food."* Instead, he peered into the refrigerator. "Cream cheese and white wine. I can do something with that."

At his request, Erica took out cooking oil and salt. As she handed them to him, her smooth fingers crossed his roughened ones, setting off a spark of electricity.

She gave a little jump. "Ow."

"Didn't really hurt."

"It startled me." As he reached past her, she backed out of range. Still nervous or unusually self-protective. Or both.

"Where are your cooking pots?" Lock asked.

"In here somewhere. Help yourself."

As she moved aside, he began opening cabinets, and discovered a wealth of high quality pots and pans that gleamed like new. "You can't tell me you bought these at a thrift store."

"Wedding presents," she said. "My friends greatly over-estimated my interest in cooking."

He ran water into a large pot for pasta. "Your ex-husband wasn't domestic, I gather."

"That depends on your definition of domestic. He had a great appreciation for beds. Unfortunately, most of them belonged to other women," Erica said.

"You've skewered him with a clean thrust. Neatly done." After setting the water to boil, Lock checked the fridge again. The freezer yielded a bag of broccoli and cauliflower, which he put into another pot. While he might exist mostly on chips and takeout himself, Lock enjoyed cooking on occasion. And he considered this an occasion.

"You could use the microwave," Erica said from the corner where she'd retreated.

"Microwaved vegetables turn out rubbery," he retorted.

"Aren't they supposed to be rubbery?"

"Not on my watch." Lock located chicken broth, nutmeg, cayenne and flour for thickening. He could combine these with the cream cheese and wine to make a light version of Alfredo sauce.

Erica slid by him, her soft curves brushing Lock's side, and circled the far end of the counter. Even though she'd barely touched him, his body hardened instinctively. Thank goodness he was turned away.

"You ever been married?" She slid onto one of the stools and sat watching him.

"Never came close." He knew himself too well to allow a relationship to pass the point of no return. "Had a few girlfriends, but they were smart enough to figure out I'm basically a loner." *And if they didn't, I was out the door before they could spring the trap.*

"Then you'll appreciate that I am, too," Erica said.

He dismissed as condescending the glib response that popped up, that she was too pretty to be a loner. Erica deserved better. "Guess that gives us something in common."

"Aside from jogging and knowing Patty Denny."

"And living in Safe Harbor, California."

"Wow, we must be twins separated at birth," she said.

"No doubt." Despite the light exchange, it crossed Lock's mind that if Erica hadn't come from Boston, her remark might have hit close to the truth. One of the problems with being adopted and knowing nothing about your biological family was that you couldn't be sure who you were related to.

Someday he ought to finish the inquiries he'd started

into the identity of his birth mother. She most likely lived somewhere around here. That prospect had bugged Lock ever since Mike proposed his moving back here and buying a half interest in the agency.

Yet meeting her would mean confronting some very unpleasant issues. And possibly unleashing more anger than he was ready to deal with.

Lock was mixing the flour with the liquids when he remembered another ingredient for his dish. "Got Parmesan?"

"Up there." Erica pointed to a cupboard on his right.

"I was hoping for fresh," he admitted as he fetched it.

"Picky, picky."

"Most women admire my taste."

"Most women obviously let you get away with far too much." With lips parted, Erica awaited his response. Her mouth would fit beautifully against his, Lock noted. If he leaned across the counter, she might tense for a moment, but then...

Cut that out.

"Plates?" he asked, and answered his own question by opening another cupboard. While the matched service for four might also have come from her wedding, a few chips testified that it had seen plenty of use. "Butterflies. Do I sense a theme?"

"They've always appealed to me. I'm not sure why." From a drawer on her side of the counter, Erica produced silverware and paper napkins. "I suppose I should have outgrown them, now that I'm thirty-one."

"Such an advanced age," Lock murmured.

"I keep hoping I've at least matured enough not to make any more stupid choices, like marrying my ex."

"I wish I could say I haven't made any stupid mistakes since I turned thirty-one, or thirty-five, for that matter."

Setting down the plates, Lock stirred the spaghetti into boiling water.

"Any tips on aging gracefully?" Erica teased.

"Don't pick up girls in parks. But then, who wants to age gracefully?"

She laughed. "It's a good thing I don't want kids, or I suppose I'd be hearing the tick-tick-tick of my biological clock."

"Most women seem to." He'd always shied away from women who expressed a desire to become mothers. Then last summer in Flagstaff he'd enjoyed coaching a softball team of underprivileged kids, many of whom lacked fathers. Lock supposed that someday he might enjoy the parenting experience. Not anytime soon, though.

"Spare me." Erica made a face. "I'll leave the baby making to my patients, thank you."

"I didn't mean while you're single," he said. "That would be tough."

She tossed back her hair. There was none of that self-conscious fluffing of her locks as he'd seen some women do, just a natural way of moving that kept him aware of her femininity. "Raising a child is totally demanding. Your life isn't your own anymore. Plus they cost a fortune, and you have to worry about them every minute. I'm just too selfish. Does that turn you off?"

"Does what?"

"My not wanting kids."

Lock had always assumed that if he did marry and have children, their mother would provide the main day-to-day supervision. He'd never considered how that might feel from her perspective.

"Nope." He stirred the drained pasta into the white sauce, relishing the scents of nutmeg, Parmesan and cream cheese. "Nothing about you turns me off."

Erica looked pleased. While he knew better than to assume that meant an open invitation, Lock was enjoying the undercurrents. The tantalizing buzz. The stirrings that might lead to…

He'd better hightail it out of here as soon as they finished eating, he thought as he carried their plates of pasta and vegetables to the small table.

Erica poured white wine into stemmed glasses. "Thank you," she said. "This is lovely."

"You're welcome." Lock eased into a dark wood chair and stretched his legs until his sock-clad feet touched hers. The cozy contact sent a wave of pleasure simmering up his body.

Dangerous territory.

"Put your arm out," she commanded.

"Beg pardon?"

"A toast isn't a toast unless you link arms."

"You're right." They leaned toward each other and linked arms. This close, her soft breath tickled his neck.

Erica raised her glass. "To picking up girls in parks."

"Especially on their birthday." Lock's cheek nearly touched hers as he bent to take a sip. Her nearness gave him such a heady sensation, the wine might as well have been whiskey.

"Delicious." Her eyes took on intriguing green depths beneath starry brown flecks.

Abruptly, a loud rumble vibrated through the room. With his free hand, Lock gripped the table to steady it. He'd grown up in Southern California and took quakes, if that's what this was, in stride.

Erica jerked away, spilling wine on the table and tipping her chair. She barely avoided going over backward.

"I…" Her pupils dilated, and when he reached over and caught her wrist, it felt cold beneath his touch. From outside, he heard another rumble, followed by several thumps. Someone must be wheeling a heavy piece of furniture down the staircase.

"It isn't a quake," Lock said. "Just one of your neighbors."

Erica didn't seem to hear. She'd gone ashen, and her breath was coming fast. The trauma from that accident ten years ago not only hadn't faded, it had festered. In that moment he resolved not to leave until he made sure she was all right—no matter how long it took. Or how great the danger to his self-control.

Chapter Four

Erica couldn't stop shaking, and all because of someone moving furniture. But even though she came up with a rationale that should have reassured her—*your blood sugar's dropped for lack of food*—the terror seized her again.

Pounding pulse. Numb fingers. A sense of impending doom. If this had happened to another woman, she'd have summoned the paramedics to treat a possible heart attack. But in her case, the symptoms added up to something quite different.

Lock lifted her from the chair and carried her to the sofa. "You're having a panic attack."

"I...know." Erica's teeth chattered as he sank down with her on his lap, enclosed in his arms. Leaning against him, she let the steady thrum of his heart calm her. "This is embarrassing."

"You said the accident happened ten years ago. Was that on your birthday?" His fingers stroked her hair.

She nodded.

"Ever talk to anyone about it?" he asked.

"The police. When it happened." The shakes intensified at the memory of sitting in the hospital corridor, talking to a uniformed officer. He'd been cool, professional and remote as he took her statement. The air had felt as cold as the February chill outside. Physically, Erica had suffered only bruises and cuts. Inside, she'd been plunged into icy darkness.

Jordan was dead. He'd died shielding her.

"What about afterward?" There was a slight rasp to Lock's voice. "Did you get counseling?"

"My family dealt with problems on our own." But they hadn't really dealt with anything. Had never dealt with Jordan's drug use, and after his death had simply retreated into their shells.

"Tell me what happened."

Around Erica, the shadows lengthened. She swallowed hard.

"Let it out." Lock wasn't asking; he was ordering. Somehow, that helped.

She concentrated on the circle of light from a table lamp and the warmth of Lock's body. "Jordan picked me up at nursing school to take me to dinner for my birthday. It wasn't till he nearly hit a shuttle bus that I realized he was high."

"Your brother had a drug problem?"

"He started experimenting in college." An image of Jordan's dancing eyes and quick laugh flashed into her mind. He'd had a gift for winning hearts, including his kid sister's. "He smoked marijuana. A lot."

"No hard stuff?" Lock asked.

"Not as far as I know."

"How did your parents respond?" he probed.

"They argued. With him and with each other." Their mother had insisted that she'd tried pot in college, too, and she'd turned out okay. Their father, a trust attorney, had pointed out that marijuana was illegal, and had become more potent since those days.

They hadn't insisted on treatment or acknowledged that their son's life was careening off course, even when he dropped out of graduate school and gave up his dream of becoming a research biologist. *He'll outgrow this phase. Once he gets a job, a girlfriend, a goal in life, he'll be fine.* How many times had Erica heard those excuses?

"You said he hit a bus?" Lock prompted.

"No. He missed it." She had suggested pulling over, but her brother kept driving. "Jordan started weaving in and out of traffic, and I could smell marijuana. When he ran a red light, I thought we'd get stopped, but no such luck."

"Go on."

There'd been a couple of near misses, corners taken with a screech of brakes, angry shouts and gestures from other drivers. "We were coming up on an intersection when the light turned red. He stomped on the gas pedal and laughed like it was a great joke. The next thing I knew, we were spinning around and he threw himself over me."

"You weren't wearing seat belts?" Lock asked.

"I was, but not Jordan, and the air bags didn't inflate. I think he'd set them off before and never fixed them."

"And then?"

"He whispered, 'Live well.' That's the last thing he ever said." Tears coursed down her cheeks.

"What about the people in the other car?"

She'd always been grateful that the crash hadn't claimed anyone else. "We hit a panel truck. The driver had a few contusions, that's all."

Lock rocked her gently. "How long were you trapped in the car with your brother on top of you?"

"I'm not sure." She'd either blacked out or erased that memory. "It couldn't have been long."

"Did you have nightmares?"

"Yes. I still do." She wiped her tears on the sleeve of

her jogging suit. "He wouldn't have been there if it weren't for my birthday."

Lock's arms tightened around her. "You honestly think you're even a little bit to blame?"

"At one level, no." Erica had told herself that, many times. "But my father said…"

"Your father said what?" Lock demanded after she stopped.

She'd overheard the angry remark at the hospital. "Dad told Mom I should have noticed Jordan wasn't fit to drive."

"What did he expect you to do about it?" Lock muttered.

"Stop him." To Erica, her voice sounded small, like a child's. Sometimes she felt that way when she thought about her big brother.

"Seems like your parents were part of the problem."

"They didn't encourage Jordan to use drugs," she pointed out.

"But they failed to hold him responsible for his actions. How dare your father even hint that you were at fault!" Lock said in an offended tone. "That's typical of an enabler."

Erica wondered if he was speaking from experience. "This sounds personal."

He rested his forehead against her temple, as if he could merge their thoughts. "My adoptive parents were drug users. They always found someone else to blame for their problems. And you know where they learned to do that? From their own parents."

"Your grandparents used drugs, too?"

"My mother's mother abused alcohol. And she refused to hear any criticism of her precious daughter." His chest rose and fell heavily. "She had the nerve to say that the responsibility of raising a child put too much stress on her poor little girl. That was when I was eight, right before the police hauled my mom off to jail and sent me to foster care. By then, my dad was long gone."

"Did your grandmother try to take you in?"

"As far as I know, she never offered." Lock blew out a long breath. "It infuriates me that you've carried a burden of guilt about your brother."

"What about you?" Erica said. "You must be carrying a burden, too. Why else would you still be so angry?"

He drew his head back a few inches. "That's a conversation for another time. This is your turn to get sympathy."

Lock couldn't fool her. He was avoiding the subject because of the pain. "That bad, huh?" She kissed his cheek.

"Worse." He tried to toss off the word with a smile, but his voice caught.

"I understand that darkness. It becomes a part of you." Erica had never shared this before with anyone. "Some people think that if you focus on positive thoughts, you can banish the pain. You might bury it for a while, but it hangs on."

"I got some therapy four years later, after I found the right foster family," Lock said raggedly. "It helped, to a point."

She ran her hand over the emerging bristle on his jaw. "I'm tired of dwelling on the past. I want to feel alive, right now."

He raised her palm to his lips. "Well, if it helps, I'm definitely starting to feel alive."

Erica was, too, in places that hadn't stirred since her husband's betrayal. Now her hunger grew as, beneath her, Lock's body stiffened against her sensitive core. His mouth covered hers, parting her lips with heated urgency.

Her breast pressed against his chest, the excitement buoying Erica. Eagerly, she unfastened his shirt and stroked his muscular chest. Deft hands lifted her jersey and sports bra over her head.

"Smooth move," she was saying when his lips found a nipple, drawing a startled gasp and sending desire arrowing through her. Her back arched in invitation.

Lock shifted her off his lap and onto her side, then stretched out beside her. "You like smooth moves, do you?"

"I love them," Erica said breathlessly, and reached to unbuckle his belt.

"You've got a few yourself." Eyes half-closed, he lifted his body and poised above her while she freed him from his fastenings. His arousal was glorious to look at. Erica's center turned liquid, and when he stripped away her pants and undergarments, she was ready for him, feeling as if the sun had come out, thawing the fertile earth after a cold winter.

"Whoa. Not planning to be a mommy, remember?" He sat back, found his wallet and extracted a condom.

Erica couldn't believe she'd overlooked protection. She'd almost forgotten what it was like to sleep with a man who wasn't her husband. During her marriage she'd been on the pill, and hadn't been with anyone since then.

She helped stretch the condom over his shaft. "You're one beautiful guy."

"You ain't seen nothin' yet," Lock teased.

"Prove it," Erica returned.

"With pleasure."

She fell back, unable to think of anything but Lock as he caressed and parted her thighs. When his hardness slid inside, strength flowed from him into her. They merged into a river, sweeping away branches and rocks, old obstacles, old fears. Erica had always held a part of herself in reserve with men, even her husband, but not now. Not with Lock.

His rhythm intensified, sending waves of pleasure through her. She had never imagined she was capable of such abandon. Above her, he pumped faster, wildly, until with a cry he exploded inside her. His final thrusts fused them in a moment of pure ecstasy.

Warmth enveloped Erica as he eased down onto the couch and they nestled side by side. If not for a grumbling reminder from her stomach that she needed to eat, she'd have preferred never to move again.

Reluctantly, she nudged him. "Time to get up."

"Do we have to?" Lock asked playfully.

"I'm hungry."

"Already?"

"Not that way. Dibs on the bathroom." Erica wriggled free of their entanglement.

"Is this the thanks I get?" Lock batted lazy blue eyes at her.

"I won't be long." Off she went, contentment enveloping her.

Tomorrow, there would be loose ends and ramifications to tidy up. With relationships, there always were. Tonight, she had no intention of thinking about any of that.

HE OUGHT TO FEEL GUILTY, or at least worried, Lock mused as he lay bathed in the afterglow. He'd kept an important secret from Erica, and he'd probably violated private-detective ethics, although he'd already turned in his report. Now, if this had happened at their first meeting…well, that *would* have presented a conflict.

No sense dwelling on what hadn't occurred. He was much too happy about what had.

The connection he'd sensed hadn't been an illusion,

after all. He'd felt it even more strongly while they made love. Something about her resonated with him, as if they'd been singing the same song all their lives and just discovered how well they blended.

He wanted more of that. How much more remained to be discovered. While Lock was basically a loner, Erica didn't give off any desperate-to-tie-him-down vibes. They suited each other. He could picture more lovemaking and fun times ahead without the pressure of her wanting a commitment or a family. What more could a guy ask?

The click of the bathroom door opening reminded him that he ought to be stirring. He reached to remove the condom.

Something was wrong. He stared down in dismay.

It had torn. Damn.

Most likely it meant nothing. What were the odds? Lock had taken a few chances in his romantic past, and to his knowledge none had resulted in children. But as he grabbed his clothes and ducked past Erica, he had to admit his rosy scenario of a few minutes ago might be facing a snag.

A big one.

Chapter Five

Erica hummed as she reheated their dinners in the microwave. Her body seemed to murmur along with the melody, which she recognized as one of Dr. T's favorites—"Oh, What a Beautiful Morning" from the musical *Oklahoma!*

How saccharine could she get? Still, she felt an unaccustomed lilt to her movements as she set the warm plates on the table.

Her earlier shakiness was long gone. While she had no illusions about recovering from Jordan's death on the basis of one conversation or one episode of transcendent sex, for now the pain had receded. It had been replaced by something new, something too sensitive and fresh to analyze.

Let matters unfold at their own pace. She just hoped Lock wasn't the love-'em-and-leave-'em type, but if he was, she could handle that.

Despite her attempt at detachment, Erica's spirits lifted when he sauntered into view, shirt rumpled in defiance of his attempt to tuck it into his pants, and corded forearms visible below rolled-up sleeves.

"Dinner's ready," she said cheerfully. "Again."

"Thanks for heating it up." He held her chair for her. "Although I doubt the pasta will be quite as tasty."

"Parmesan hides a multitude of sins." She'd cleaned

up the mess she'd made and poured fresh glasses of wine. Lucky that she preferred white, since red would have left a stain on the rug.

They ate in what seemed to her a comfortable silence. Absorbed in her food, Erica didn't register the tension in Lock until his stiff fingers knocked over the saltshaker.

She reached to right it. When their hands brushed, he jerked away.

Disappointment dimmed her mood. Ignoring the salt, she regarded him steadily. "If you're concerned that I'm the clingy type, don't be."

"What?" He rotated his empty wineglass absently.

"If you break that, you pay for it." She hoped the joke would lighten the mood, but he merely set the glass down. "If you're going to bolt for the door, don't forget your shoes and jacket. I'd hate to have to send them by way of Patty."

Was that guilt in his expression? Erica couldn't figure out this guy. For heaven's sake, she'd practically given him permission to dump her. What could be bothering him?

He patted his mouth with his napkin and took a deep breath. "The condom broke."

"What?"

Lock didn't repeat the statement. Obviously, she'd heard it. She was just having trouble grasping the implications.

"Exactly how long had that thing been in your wallet?" Erica asked. "Don't tell me you bought it out of a vending machine at a rest stop."

"I don't remember, and no," he answered in a level tone. "Let's move past affixing blame, okay?"

She hadn't meant to do that. "Sorry."

"The odds are fairly low that you'll…you know."

"I'm a nurse in a fertility program. You can say the word *pregnant* around me." Hearing her sarcastic tone,

Erica waved a hand apologetically. "Sorry again. My responses tend to be defensive."

"I understand."

The condom broke. She wished he could take back those words. Oh, for pity's sake, that wasn't the issue. Why had she been such an idiot? Why had she imagined that a few minutes of lust were worth the risk?

"You're right," she said into the silence. "The odds are low. I work with women who try for years to get pregnant. Even under normal circumstances, it takes a few months."

"Nature has a quirky sense of humor." Lock stacked her empty plate atop his. "Whatever happens, you can count on me. We'll get through this together."

Why was he acting as if they were a couple? "I barely know you." Erica ignored the little voice reminding her that she should have thought of that sooner.

"It looks like we're going to know each other a lot better," he said.

Suddenly she longed to be alone. Solitude meant being free of other people's emotions, alone to be churlish and angry without having to act polite.

"I'm a big girl. I can take the consequences of my actions." Getting to her feet, Erica grabbed the plates and silverware and made her getaway to the kitchen. "If you don't mind, I'm tired and I have to be up early tomorrow."

"You work on Saturdays?" Lock asked.

"I put in an extra half day if Dr. Tartikoff schedules surgery. And he usually does." At the sink, she set the plates to soak.

"Erica, are you kicking me out?"

"Not exactly."

"But if I stick around for dessert, you might throw it at my head?" Lock said.

She turned to face him. "Okay, yes. You should leave."

"Why?" he asked. "We're equally involved in this situation."

How typical of a guy to think that way. "I'm the one who'll swell up like a balloon and go through nine months of discomfort and hours of agony if I'm pregnant." She didn't mean to rail at him, but being put in this situation infuriated her. "Lock, I appreciate that you mean well, but this is my problem. *If* there's a problem."

"I want to help."

"I don't need help." Why hadn't he been more careful about the condom? It was too late for him to change anything now. "This is probably all unnecessary. So don't worry about it."

His jaw worked. At last he gave a reluctant nod. "Promise to call me when you know what's what." He handed her a business card bearing his name and phone number under the logo of Fact Hunter Investigations.

"All right." She put the card in a drawer under the counter, between a deck of playing cards and a tray of pens and pencils.

They regarded each other across the counter. To Erica, it felt like the Great Wall of China. "Want a ride to your car now?" he asked. "Or I could stop by in the morning."

She'd forgotten about that. "I'll get up early and walk."

"That's a long way."

"It's only a mile and a half."

His shrug conceded defeat. "You have my number. And, Erica?"

She watched warily as he put on his jacket and shoes. "Yes?"

"Happy birthday." With a rueful smile, out he went.

Erica flipped the bolt behind him. What was that old saying about closing the barn door after the horse had escaped? *Or, rather, after you let him inside in the first place.*

Turning, she pressed her back to the door and sought comfort in the familiarity of the room. There was the couch she'd lovingly recovered and refinished after she found it, frayed and scuffed, at an end-of-the-college-year sale in Cambridge. A couple of stained-glass lamps from a pawn shop, the round table from an estate sale in Brookline, the antique frame for which she'd had a mirror cut to size. This was her home, sheltering and filled with the personal power she'd sworn never to yield to anyone.

A sense of calm settled over Erica. As she'd told Lock, she could deal just fine with whatever developed.

THWACK! THE WHITE BALL shot across the pool table and sent colored balls skimming over the green felt. As Lock moved into position for his next shot, he tried in vain to tune out Mike's voice, talking on the phone in the depths of their rented house.

"Thanks, Mom," his brother was saying. "Okay, now tell me about Grandma's diabetes. Was that type 1 or type 2?"

Why on earth did the guy care? Lock wondered grumpily, and took an angle shot. Two balls kissed, knocking one a few inches out of the way and pocketing the other. He made his way around the table, gauging his best bet for scoring.

He wasn't sure why it seemed so important to tune up his game. Sure, he and his brother had a friendly rivalry with some of Mike's old police buddies, who occasionally dropped by to enjoy the pool table that had come with the rest of the furnishings. Mostly, though, Lock needed to blow off energy, and on a rainy March evening, after a long day at work, he didn't feel like going for a run.

These past five weeks, he'd done plenty of jogging, everywhere but City Hall Park. Giving Erica her space seemed the honorable thing to do. Finally, he'd left a message on her cell phone, figuring she ought to know by now whether she was pregnant. She hadn't responded to that message or a second one, either.

Erica's silence didn't keep her out of his thoughts. Their time together had replayed through his mind countless times. Finally Lock had figured out why gazing into her eyes gave him the sense of staring into his own soul.

The two of them were emotional twins. Both had been emotionally abandoned—in his case literally, by his birth mother and his adoptive parents; in her case by parents who'd turned a cold shoulder when she'd needed them most and later by her creep of a husband. Now he and Erica had the same instinct for pulling away from relationships, the same prickly insistence on independence and the same fierce resistance against being caged.

Except this time, he didn't feel like ducking out. Not yet, anyway.

"Was Grandma's heart attack related to the diabetes?" Mike's voice echoed down the hallway. Hadn't he ever heard of closing the door? "No, Mom, I'm not having problems. Like I told you, I have to fill out a medical history."

Was this a new insurance requirement? Lock had been astonished at the mountains of paperwork required to operate a business in California.

If he had to fill out a family medical history, he'd be done in a minute. What little he knew came from the papers that had followed him from the adoption agency through several foster homes. Mother's age at birth: seventeen. Her marital status: single. Her health: good. Her occupation: student. Nothing about his father. No idea if his parents or grandparents had suffered from diabetes, heart disease, leprosy or beriberi.

"I'm afraid it doesn't work that way. I'll never find out, so you won't, either." Mike's conversation with his mother appeared to have moved to a new topic. "What's the big deal? Marianne's only thirty. I'm sure she'll get married and have kids one of these days. And how about Lourdes? She's got two and Denzel has one that we know of. Also, aren't Fatima and her husband expecting?"

Lock set down his pool cue. He couldn't concentrate while his brain was puzzling over this one-sided conversation. Marianne was Mike's biological sister. Lourdes and Denzel had been among the foster kids who came and went during Lock's time with the Aarons, while Fatima had joined the flock later. Although many had lost touch over the years, those three, along with their various spouses and kids, and Lock joined the dinner table at Thanksgiving and Christmas.

If he understood correctly, Mike was reassuring his mother about grandchildren. But what did this have to do with his medical history or that odd statement: "I'll never find out"?

After racking the balls, Lock went into the kitchen, his shoes scuffing the worn linoleum. They were out of tortilla chips, he discovered. No cookies, either. Mike had taken the last turn at shopping, and all he'd bought for snacking appeared to be fruit.

Lock was finishing a banana when his brother showed up, sandy hair tousled as if he'd been running his fingers through it. Conversations with Nina Aaron tended to do that to her son.

As for Lock, he enjoyed her probing into the details of his personal life, because it showed that she cared. Recently, though, he'd steered their discussions onto safer topics, such as how well he'd done on the two-hour private-investigators exam. That had been an ordeal, covering laws and regulations and civil and criminal liability, as well as evidence handling, undercover investigations and surveillance. He'd passed with flying colors and earned his license.

From a bowl on the counter, Mike snatched an apple and bit into it. "What was all that about?" Lock asked him.

"What was all what?" he responded through a full mouth. "Did you wash these?"

"You bought 'em," Lock said. "Besides, washing fruit is for sissies."

Mike pretended to lob the apple at him, then took another bite.

"Next time, get chips," Lock said.

"Next time's on you. You can buy whatever you want. Just get healthy stuff for me." A few more bites, and the apple core made a clean arc into the wastebasket. His brother opened the fridge and stared at the shelves. Beer versus juice. Tough choice. His hand moved back and forth several times before alighting on the juice.

"You must have had your physical," Lock surmised. "High blood sugar?"

"No." Mike collected a tumbler from the top shelf in the cabinet. Easy reach for him.

"Why the health kick? And why all the questions about your grandmother?"

"Quit being so nosy."

"You hired me to be nosy. So speak." When Lock had first arrived at the Aarons' home, he'd been a scared twelve-year-old who hid his feelings behind a defensive wall of anger. Gradually, guided by his new family's combination of strictness and love, he'd begun to trust them enough to open up. Now, Lock couldn't imagine *not* prying into his brother's business.

Mike leaned his tall frame against the counter. "I've applied to become a sperm donor."

Lock blurted the first thing that came to mind. "Money isn't *that* tight."

A rude noise greeted this remark.

"It can't pay all that much, anyway." Lock stretched his leg and massaged the thigh. Although it hurt less these days, it still felt tight.

"I'm not doing it for the money, which is about a hundred dollars per specimen, if you must know," Mike said.

"Then why?"

His brother's blue-gray eyes fixed on the ceiling. "Does it matter?"

"It must matter to you, or you wouldn't go through this," Lock stated.

"I'm helping women and couples have families. Isn't that enough of a motive?"

"No."

Mike gulped the juice and set the glass in the sink. "The idea's fascinated me ever since I heard the hospital was opening a sperm bank."

"Does this have to do with Patty's husband working there?" Lock queried.

"He's an embryologist. Different department," Mike said. "Okay, here's the deal. After spending years helping out with foster kids, I have no desire to be a father. But I'm arrogant enough to want to pass along my gene pool."

Hence the health kick and the medical history. "What if your kids come looking for you someday? Or a woman demands child support?"

"There are laws protecting my rights and theirs." Those issues didn't appear to trouble him. "Think about it. I come from a high-achieving family with no history of drug or alcohol abuse. All but one of my grandparents lived into their eighties in good health. Why not pass those genes to another generation?"

Lock had a ready answer. "I can't imagine knowing you've got a kid out there, or maybe several kids, that you'll never meet. Wouldn't you wonder every time you see a child whether it might be yours?"

"I think having a lot of kids would be cool, as long as I don't have to take care of them," Mike returned evenly.

Surely he hadn't weighed all the implications. "Suppose you get married. How do you think your wife will feel about this?"

"I tried marriage. Didn't work for me." Mike's marriage had fallen apart after he'd caught his wife having an affair. In the years since then, he'd dated only casually.

Lock wasn't finished. "You grew up with foster kids. You saw what being thrown away does to them."

"I'm not throwing anyone away. I'll be making a donation to women who badly want a family," he replied smoothly.

"You have no idea what it's like not knowing where you came from or what your real parents were like!"

His brother fixed him with a steely look. "If you're hung up about your genetic parents, bro, why don't you check them out? You're a detective. Shouldn't be hard to find your birth mother."

"I've considered it."

"Consider it harder. Now quit bugging me." Mike propelled himself away from the counter. "I'm going to hit the treadmill."

That meant an hour of mechanized creaking and churning next to Lock's bedroom. If he'd had any plans for hitting the sack early, he could forget about them.

Grabbing the laptop he'd left in the den, he carried it into the living room and set it up on the coffee table. For an unguarded moment, he reflected on how totally unlike Erica's place this was, with its threadbare couch and chairs facing a giant TV screen. Not even the most dedicated bargain hunter would bother to refinish this scarred coffee table, decorated only by mug-size rings and the scuff marks of countless shoes.

Erica. He saw again the defensiveness in her crossed arms and tight expression after she'd learned she might be pregnant. Why was she so stubbornly insistent about standing on her own? Well, that was her right, just as it was Mike's right to fill the world with his offspring if the sperm bank accepted his application.

As he'd said, he wasn't throwing anyone away. Rationally, Lock knew his birth mother probably hadn't intended to do that, either. But why *had* she given him up?

On the internet, he clicked on an adoption search site he'd bookmarked during his convalescence. Being seriously wounded made a guy reflect on life, death and major unanswered questions, and he'd taken the first steps toward locating his birth mother, before deciding he wasn't ready.

He'd listed the little he knew about the circumstances of his relinquishment, including the agency involved, along with his birth date. Although he'd been born in Orange County, he had no idea at which hospital. It would have been easier if he could have talked to his adoptive parents, but his father had vanished after their divorce, and although Lock's mother had been released from prison while he was with the Aarons, she'd made no attempt to see him.

He'd heard that she'd died of a drug overdose not long afterward. A few years later, her own mother had passed on, ironically leaving no heirs except her unwanted adoptive grandson. The inheritance had paid for college and his share of Fact Hunter Investigations, with a tidy sum left over.

How could his birth mother have entrusted him to such unstable people? Sure, there'd been a few tender moments that ached in his memory: his adoptive mom singing him to sleep, his father teaching Lock's five-year-old self to bat a ball in the backyard. He'd loved them with all his young heart, and they hadn't cared enough about him to put their lives in order.

Lock shifted his attention to the website, which allowed both adoptive children and birth parents to input their information. They could then learn if there were people whose parameters matched, without names or other identifying data. Instead, you could, if you chose, agree to have your email address forwarded.

Three women were listed as having given birth to male babies in Orange County on the same date and had relinquished them for adoption at the same agency. Since he'd posted his information months earlier, none of the mothers had forwarded their addresses to Lock. Presumably, they were waiting for him to make the first move.

His fingers hung over the keyboard. All he had to do was click in the right spot and he'd be on the road to answering his questions.

Or opening Pandora's box. He'd read on chat sites about painful experiences, as well as joyous reunions. There was no guarantee his birth mom hadn't been a druggie, too. Or that she wouldn't cling to him obsessively, or have other children who would resent him.

Alternatively, Lock reflected, he might ruin a nice woman's fantasy about the picture-perfect life her son had led with his adoptive family. Most adoptions worked out well, after all. Plus his lingering resentment was likely to spill over and poison whatever chance they had of forming a bond.

He logged off and closed the laptop. What was that old saying about letting sleeping dogs lie? In this case, it might be more like a pack of wolves.

Better to let them snooze than to end up provoking an experience he might forever regret.

Chapter Six

Although Erica assisted surgeons other than Dr. T when the schedule required, she didn't usually enjoy the experience. Not being accustomed to their preferences regarding instruments and procedures, she couldn't achieve her usual standard of near perfection. Also, she missed his dry wit and easy banter.

But one afternoon in March, when she looked at the board and saw that she was set to assist Dr. Paige Brennan next, she felt a touch of relief.

Dr. T hadn't been very pleasant that morning. Both twins had come down with bad colds, and he'd worried aloud about the possibility of them developing something more serious. After listening to him recount in excruciating detail how he'd spent the night suctioning their little noses and monitoring their temperatures, Erica had tried to change the subject, only to receive a sharp response.

Perhaps she shouldn't have asked for hints about the announcement he was scheduled to make at a staff meeting later in the week. But she'd figured she deserved some advance notice, since it likely involved the proposed contest for which they'd been tossing around ideas for weeks. In addition to boosting morale and gaining publicity, he'd mentioned his goal of encouraging doctors to be more aggressive in using the latest fertility techniques, and he'd liked her suggestion of offering a reward. So she hadn't expected him to snap, "In case this hasn't occurred to you, Nurse, it's called a surprise announcement because it's supposed to be a surprise."

"Yes, Doctor," she'd said as evenly as she could. Given her edgy mood these past few days, she figured she deserved a gold star for keeping her cool. But doctors didn't give nurses credit for that sort of thing.

As she downed a power bar to settle her queasy stomach, Erica missed the boost she normally got from coffee. But the stuff tasted bitter, no doubt due to a flood of hormones. The awareness that she couldn't postpone taking a pregnancy test much longer didn't help her mood, either.

Delaying the news meant putting off having to decide what to do when the results came back positive, as she was pretty sure they would. For all Lock's promises of aid, she was in this alone. Her body, her future.

The fact that he'd phoned a few times didn't reassure her. The guy must be trying to learn whether he was off the hook. Once she took the test, Erica supposed she'd have to call him back. And say what, exactly?

Yeah, we had a great time. You reminded me of how wonderful it can be to connect with a man.

Reminded wasn't even the operative word. She'd never had that strong a sense of bonding with her husband.

It scared the hell out of her. Far better to keep her distance, physically and in every other way. Falling in love led to pain and disappointment, and she'd had more than enough of those.

She went to scrub in. Thank goodness for the orderly, focused nature of surgery.

Erica had worked with Dr. Brennan before and liked the obstetrician's no-nonsense manner. Nearly six feet tall, with dramatic red hair, Paige had joined the staff to fill in during Nora Kendall Franco's extended maternity leave. No one seemed to know what Paige would do when Nora returned, but that didn't appear to be imminent.

Today's surgery was a hysterectomy on a woman in her thirties seeking relief from endometriosis. Fortunately, she already had two children.

"I don't suppose you can tell us what Dr. Tartikoff plans to announce, can you?" Paige asked once the surgery was under way.

"He nearly bit her head off when she asked this morning," said Rod Vintner. The anesthesiologist had witnessed that unfortunate exchange.

"Dr. T was in a bad mood," Erica explained. "His kids are sick." No matter how irritated she might feel, she didn't criticize her doctor to others.

"He fussed about them all morning." Rod kept an eye on the display showing the patient's heart rate and blood pressure. "I didn't even get a chance to tell him about my hot date last Saturday."

That sounded more interesting than runny noses and crying kids, Erica thought as she handed Dr. Brennan a scalpel. She saw the circulating nurse perk up, too.

"Pray don't keep us in suspense," Paige said.

Rod cleared his throat. "We had great vibes at dinner. Ever see the movie *Tom Jones?* That kind of dinner. Then she mentioned that she plans to get married next Valentine's Day."

"She went out on a date when she's engaged?" Erica asked in disbelief.

"Not exactly." Rod paused for dramatic effect. "She booked the hall, bought the dress, reserved the caterer and for all I know hired the band, but she doesn't have the man yet. It's kind of like baiting a trap and hoping Mr. Right will fall into it."

"Incredible," said the circulating nurse. "Even if it is nearly a year away."

Erica couldn't imagine being that presumptuous or that foolish. "What's her rationale?"

"She believes in the power of positive thinking," Rod chortled.

"That woman doesn't understand men," Dr. Brennan said. "To bait a trap, she should have used a big-screen TV and a refrigerator full of beer."

"And invited him over on Super Bowl Sunday," Erica added.

Paige laughed. "Since that's only about a week before Valentine's Day, she could drag him down the aisle before he knows what hit him."

Rod responded with a grin. "I'd better watch my back around you two."

He and Paige went on to swap observations about the failings of the opposite sex, both having had their share of disillusioning experiences. Erica would have contributed a few remarks of her own if her stomach hadn't chosen that moment to wage a rebellion. As the wave of nausea passed, she caught a concerned glance from Dr. Brennan.

Later, as they were cleaning up, the doctor addressed Erica quietly. "Are you feeling all right?"

"Just a little off."

"Are you sure?"

On the verge of insisting she was fine, Erica realized that she did need an ob-gyn. Since moving west, she'd postponed scheduling her annual physical, and hadn't yet selected a physician. Who better than someone she already knew and trusted? "I might be pregnant."

"Why don't we go over to my office and I'll give you a test?" Paige suggested.

"I can pick up a kit at the pharmacy." Another wave of nausea swept through Erica. She leaned against the wall.

"A kit won't check your vitals and answer your questions," the taller woman said as she stripped off her surgical gown. "If you don't mind my asking, is there a steady guy in the picture?"

It was too complicated to explain, so Erica simply said, "No."

"Then I recommend you have someone else with you when you get the news. Me, for instance. It's a bad idea to be standing in a bathroom with nothing but a pink stick to keep you company."

Erica felt an unexpected longing for Lock's sturdy presence. Much as she took pride in managing her own problems, she hadn't counted on her traitorous body making her feel shaky. Or on her hormone-fueled psyche longing for a shoulder to lean on.

Oh, right. Lock was the last person she should be with when she got the news. Too many issues to deal with, on top of the pregnancy itself. Paige's offer made sense, and Erica had finished her shift for the day. "Do you have time now?"

"I'll make time."

"I'll meet you there," Erica promised. "Thanks, Dr. Brennan."

"Glad to help. And look on the bright side. Pregnancy isn't the worst thing that can happen to a woman." Was that a wistful note in the other woman's voice? "See you shortly."

Half an hour later, Erica sat in an examining room in the medical building adjacent to the hospital, receiving news she really didn't want to hear.

"You're definitely pregnant." Dr. Brennan studied the

test results in the computer. "I'd put your due date at mid-November."

A rush of tears caught Erica off guard. As they streamed down her cheeks, Paige handed her a box of tissues. "I know this is tough."

Embarrassed, Erica mopped herself up. "We have so many patients who'd give anything to be in this position."

The red-haired doctor inhaled sharply. Did she long for a baby, too? According to hospital gossip, she was neither married nor dating anyone steadily.

Well, neither am I.

"You have some decisions to make," the doctor went on. "How about talking to a counselor? I can recommend someone who specializes in maternity issues."

That was exactly the advice Erica would give another woman in her situation. But to her, relying on a therapist felt like an admission of weakness. "No, thanks."

Her hand drifted to her abdomen. Impossible as it seemed, there was a baby growing in there, a tiny version of herself or Lock. Would it have his intense blue eyes or her hazel ones? And what about their personalities? She had to smile.

Paige regarded her questioningly. "What's so funny?"

"Is it possible for a baby to be born cynical?" Erica asked. "Because this one is going to inherit that trait from both sides."

"I once delivered a baby that was the spitting image of W. C. Fields. He's the comedian who said, 'A woman drove me to drink and I didn't even have the decency to thank her,'" Paige responded. "I swear, that kid's fingers were twitching as if trying to twirl a cigar. Nearly made me believe in reincarnation."

Erica laughed. "I'd like a picture of that." As for the baby inside *her,* she already had a mental picture of a little person who'd suddenly become much more than a theoretical possibility. A person with roots deep inside her genetic heritage, and Lock's. A person who deserved much better than to be brought up by an unprepared and unwilling mother.

"What's on your mind?" the doctor asked. "You just ran through half a dozen different facial expressions and I'm fresh out of ESP."

"I'm facing the fact that I have neither the temperament nor the desire to be a mom," Erica said. "I'm going to put him or her up for adoption. And the sooner I get the paperwork taken care of, the better."

"There's no hurry," Paige cautioned. "It's a big step. I really do recommend seeing a counselor."

She shrugged off the advice. "Why waste everyone's time? I'll be a lot happier if I know I'm doing this for a family who will cherish this child, and that in the end, I'll walk away a free woman."

"Very well." Dr. Brennan jotted a note in the computer. "I'll ask my nurse to give you a prescription for maternal vitamins and schedule your next appointment. You'll need blood work, too. In the meantime, I suggest you talk to Tony Franco."

"The hospital attorney?" He was also Dr. Nora Franco's brother-in-law, Erica recalled. She'd met the man a few times at staff meetings.

"He keeps a list of local adoption agencies, and he can advise you on the legalities," Paige said.

"Sounds good."

After getting dressed, Erica put in a call. Tony agreed to meet with her right away in his office on the fifth floor of the hospital.

On the short walk to the next building, she enjoyed the soft breeze and the scent of early spring flowers. Her spirits felt lighter now that she'd made her decision. The coming months might be difficult, but she could see light at the end of the tunnel. Or was that at the end of the birth canal? Erica mused.

In the administrative suite, Tony, a steady man with rust-brown hair, ushered her into his office and listened thoughtfully as Erica explained the circumstances. Although his desk bore a photo of his wife, six-year-old stepson and toddler daughter, he didn't try to talk her out of her decision. However, he raised a point she hadn't anticipated.

"You do know who the father is, correct?" Tony asked, tilting back his swivel chair. Behind him, a large window overlooked a panorama of cliffs, beach and white-flecked Pacific Ocean.

"Of course!"

"I don't mean to insult you." Tony spread his hands placatingly. "It's just that, unless he's what the courts call a 'casual inseminator,' he has a right to contest the adoption."

"He has what?" In Erica's opinion, an unmarried and essentially uninvolved father shouldn't have any rights.

Tony reached into a drawer and retrieved a document. "This is a waiver of his parental rights. He can sign it before the child is born, which would be the easiest thing, from your perspective."

"Is this absolutely necessary?"

"I'm afraid so."

That meant not only having to reveal the situation to Lock, which she'd planned to do anyway, but requesting his cooperation. "I suppose I could mail it to him," Erica muttered. "No, that's not a good idea, is it?"

"My advice is to make sure he feels respected. Courtesy goes a long way," Tony said. "If you like, I can talk to him."

Although she appreciated the offer, Erica doubted Lock would react well to hearing about this from a lawyer. "I'd better see him myself."

"If there's anything I can do, let me know." Tony spoke earnestly.

"Thanks." Taking the document, which the attorney tucked inside a protective folder, Erica rose stiffly. This infant might not be any bigger than her thumbnail, but as she crossed the thick carpet, it weighed heavily on her.

Still, what was Lock going to do? He might fuss, but in the end, he'd go along. And if he offered chocolates and massages during the pregnancy, that wouldn't be so bad, would it?

As quickly as she entertained the notion, Erica dismissed it. Once she had his signature on the paper, it would be best if they never saw each other again.

Chapter Seven

The smell of machine oil filled Lock's office, although he could see that his client had made an honest attempt at cleaning up. On their previous in-person contacts, he'd visited Phil DiDonato at his garage, but this time the mechanic had insisted on coming to him.

On the desk lay a file open to the photo Lock had provided of Phil's eleven-year-old niece smoking cigarettes with a couple teenagers. It had seemed precisely the evidence Phil needed to convince his mother that the girl needed stronger supervision than she could provide.

"When I said Kelli should live with me, Mom went ballistic." The mechanic paced the floor. Although in his mid-thirties, he had a weathered complexion, in part from riding all-terrain vehicles in the desert. "She called me a bad influence. That's crazy! I've been Kelli's surrogate dad since her father died in Iraq." He'd explained previously that her mother suffered from severe depression and couldn't take care of the girl, which was why Phil's mom had custody.

"Your mother must be concerned that her granddaughter is cutting school." Lock tried not to get personally involved in cases, but this girl looked so young and vulnerable. Her situation reminded him in some ways of his own childhood, except that she had a grandmother and an uncle who loved her. Too bad she didn't appreciate how lucky she was.

"Mom's in denial, I guess you'd say." Phil gestured with his oil-stained hands. In a frayed but clean work shirt and jeans, he was the picture of a hardworking guy at the end of a long day. "Now she's mad at me. Mom even threatened to cut me off from Kelli, which isn't fair to either of us."

"Kelli doesn't act rebellious around you?" Lock asked.

"She still likes going to the movies or bowling with her old uncle, even though she does spend part of the time texting."

If this were his niece, Lock imagined he'd crack down on that. But never having been in such a situation, he was hardly in a position to give advice.

"The longer this goes on, the worse it'll get." Phil resumed pacing. "Today it's cigarettes, tomorrow it could be drugs or sex. I figure if she lived with me, boys would think twice about messing with her."

"Still, she needs a mother figure, too." Since the grandmother had raised the girl for the past eight years, they must have a close bond, no matter how defiant Kelli acted.

"Any suggestions?"

Changing a grandmother's mind and reining in a wayward adolescent fell outside Lock's area of expertise. But without intervention, this girl was headed for serious trouble. "I know where she hangs out and who her so-called friends are. Let me keep an eye on her. I'll swing by from time to time, but not so often that she's likely to notice."

Phil cleared his throat. "If you see her involved in anything illegal, you'll call me, not the cops, right?"

"If there's immediate danger, I'd have to call them. Plus, I do have legal obligations." Lock had to be frank about that. "But that leaves a big gray area. Basically, I'm not here to sic the police on my clients or their families."

"Thanks." Phil shook hands. "I'll pay whatever it costs."

"I'll try to keep it within reason."

Lock escorted him out. At this hour, past six, the secretary had gone home and there was no sign of Patty.

Through the closed door of Mike's office, Lock heard his brother on the phone, giving his standard spiel about what they charged and what services they provided. "Mind if I ask where you got our name?" he was saying. "The Yellow Pages? Well, I'd be happy to provide you with a list of references if you'd like."

Good thing Mike spearheaded the sales end of things, because new business was essential and sales was his forte. The company had come with a list of corporate clients acquired by its retired founder, an ex-cop and ex-marine named Bruce Hunter, but they weren't enough to keep three detectives busy.

After holding open the exit door for Phil, Lock was about to retreat when he heard a light step below on the stairs, and then the mechanic say, "Excuse me, ma'am."

"I can squeeze by," a woman responded. Lock's throat tightened as he recognized the husky tone.

Erica.

Straightening, he fought back the urge to run his hand across his stubbly jaw. No time to shave, anyway.

Then it occurred to him what this must mean. Erica wouldn't bother to drop by simply to relieve his concerns.

Lock reminded himself to stay calm. Yet if he was going to be a father... It didn't seem possible. Even though he'd been turning over the idea for weeks, it now struck him as unlikely. She must have some other reason for coming.

Perhaps she'd found out he'd been spying on her? That *would* be awkward.

He stayed where he was, still holding the door open, as Erica came up the stairs. She looked crisply professional in a salmon blazer and print skirt. Despite the ironic twist to her mouth, he caught a hint of uncertainty in her eyes when she spotted him. "I didn't expect a welcome committee."

"Glad you could drop by."

"Interesting location. I never heard of Sexy Over Sixty before. Get much business from the senior crowd?" As she moved past, a trace of sweetness floated in the air.

"Sometimes," he said. "We've helped expose a couple of investment scams. And older people have cheating spouses just like younger ones." Lock's hands flexed with an impulse to touch that tumble of blond hair.

Her gaze traveled along the wall in the reception area, past the array of certificates to a framed newspaper clipping about Lock pulling two people from a burning building. "Something of a hero, are you?"

"Just doing my job."

He was about to ask what brought her here when he heard Mike say, "I'll stop by tomorrow morning at ten. Thanks for calling Fact Hunter Investigations, Mrs. Smith."

Any minute, Mike was likely to emerge, and he'd almost certainly recognize Erica from the photos Lock had shot. If he learned of their involvement, there'd be hell to pay.

"Smith?" repeated Erica. "Are people afraid to give their real names?"

"Some people actually are called Smith." Putting a gentle hand on the small of her back, Lock steered her into his office.

Had he left anything incriminating on his desk or computer screen? he wondered as he closed the door behind them. Although Lock was no longer working on the Ginnifer Moran case, he'd received an email from her this morning. She'd thanked him for his thoroughness and for preventing a marriage that would have been a disaster.

His computer monitor showed the usual array of icons. On the desk, the only thing that stood out was the photo of Phil's niece, which he swept into a folder. "Pretend you didn't see that."

"I'm not here to pry." She gripped the back of a chair, suddenly pale.

Lock hurried to her side. "Are you okay? Anything I can get you? Water or coffee?"

Growing even paler, she sank into the seat. "Just your signature on this." From her large purse, she drew a file folder and handed him a legal-looking document.

Was she seeking child support? Lock hadn't considered that possibility, but he could hardly object. Taking the paper, he read the header a couple of times before the meaning dawned. "You're asking me to waive my parental rights. Is this your subtle way of telling me you're pregnant?"

Her eyes widened. "I meant to say that first. Yes, obviously, I am."

Lock struggled for a response. Hard to find one when so many different reactions seethed inside him. Wonder. Concern. A little guilt, too, for putting her in a position she so clearly didn't want. "Are you okay?" he asked again.

"The doctor says I'm fine. I'd like to settle on an adoptive family as soon as possible." A small, determined figure, she stared at him fiercely. "I never wanted to go through a pregnancy, as you well know, but now that it's happening, I'll try to make the best of it. And this will be the best."

"For who?"

"For everybody. Especially the child."

"It didn't work out that way for me." Realizing he was crumpling the paper, Lock relaxed his grip. Why was he arguing? He couldn't force Erica to keep the baby. He wasn't even sure he wanted her to.

"I don't know why your birth mother chose those awful people, but I can assure you I'll be careful," Erica told him. "Furthermore, this isn't your decision."

He scowled at the paper. "Apparently it is, since you need my permission."

Anger flashed in her eyes. "Are you planning to spend the next eight months feeling like a bloated whale with the flu? You have a lot of nerve giving me grief over this."

Lock flinched. "I never meant to do this to you."

"Let's not get into a discussion of blame," Erica said tightly. "Sign the damn paper and you can go your merry way."

He ought to be grateful that she wanted nothing more than that. Instead, Lock kept picturing her cozy apartment, the radiance from a stained-glass lamp illuminating her face as she gazed invitingly at him. They'd found something, created something. Started a new life in a moment of ecstasy. That meant a lot.

"What's the hurry?" He wished he didn't sound so strained. Keep it casual and she might ease off, at least for now. "How soon could you select a family, anyway?"

Erica blew a tendril of hair off her cheek. "I suppose I should wait till after the first trimester, but I can start doing research now."

"What's stopping you?"

"You, you big jerk."

He gave a bark of laughter. "You don't mince words."

She fished in her purse and handed him a pen. "That's right. So sign it."

As he took the pen, Lock noticed the words printed on it: *Safe Harbor: a Place for Women and Babies.* What about fathers?

His fingers refused to do anything except return the implement. "I need a few days to process this idea. How about if I bring the paper to your place over the weekend and we can discuss it?"

"You can drop it off at the hospital on Friday. Signed." Erica handed him the folder that had protected the document. "That'll keep it safe. I'd rather you didn't reduce it to a wad."

He respected her toughness. "You'd have made a good cop."

"Too short," Erica said.

"Not necessarily." Still, he was glad her job didn't require that she put herself in danger. "Okay, Friday."

"Leave it at the front desk."

"I'd rather deliver it in person."

She sighed. "I get off work around three-thirty. Cell phones don't work in some areas, so have the desk page me."

"Sounds good." He wasn't sure why he felt so reluctant to get this over with. Maybe because he didn't want to sever his link to Erica, he supposed. But he would never use this as leverage to try to force a relationship.

Friday. Hopefully, he'd resolve his confusion by then.

She was on her feet. Lock hurried to get in a last word. "I hope you'll consider me a resource during your pregnancy. With finances, for one thing."

"I expect the adoptive family will take care of that."

"Will they run errands? Cook meals? You need to eat healthy food," he warned as he saw her out.

"What makes you think I don't?"

"I've seen your refrigerator, remember?" he was saying before realizing that they weren't alone.

Mike's grim expression warned of trouble as he addressed Erica. "Hi, I'm Mike Aaron."

"My partner." Lock saw no reason to detail their relationship further. "Mike, this is—"

"Nice to meet you," Erica interrupted. "I'm not a client, so let's leave my name out of this." Her frosty civility was more than a match for Mike's. "I was on my way out." With a glance at Lock that said, *Friday, and don't screw this up,* she was off.

Mike waited until enough time passed for her to be out of earshot. "What was that about?"

Lock saw no point in ducking the question. "That was the woman I was investigating, Erica Benford. She's pregnant."

To someone who didn't know Mike, his reaction might have gone unnoticed. Lock, however, registered it in the twitch of a jaw muscle and a watchful, wary tension. "This is the woman you reported didn't sleep around."

"Check." Lock awaited the next question.

"And who refused your advances."

"Check."

"Who, according to your report, leads a nunlike existence, nursing the afflicted while remaining chaste."

Lock inclined his head in the affirmative.

"Let me see if I got this straight," Mike continued drily. "Ms. Benford has undergone a miraculous conception and dropped by our office because she couldn't resist sharing the news with a man whose advances she rebuffed."

"Also because I'm the father," Lock conceded.

Mike dropped the sarcastic tone. "You do understand that you have committed a whole raft of…I don't even know what to call them. Ethical breaches."

"It isn't what it looks like." Lock didn't rush to explain. His brother was not his boss.

"Well?" An edge of irritation testified to Mike's fraying patience.

"It happened *after* I filed my report," he said. "We ran into each other and I pulled her out of the path of a car. She was upset, and I did my best to comfort her."

"That's your idea of comfort?"

"What better?"

Mike glanced toward the outer office, empty now that Erica had disappeared. "If she's shaking you down for child support, I hope you plan on running a DNA test."

Well, that was a change in attitude. "No, I don't."

"Come on, bro. I'm pretty damn ticked off. Our client could sue if she decides we misinformed her. But that doesn't mean I'll let you get played."

"Erica asked me to waive my parental rights so she can give up the baby for adoption. Does that sound like she's shaking me down?"

Mike shrugged. "Watch yourself. This lady may not be the model of innocence you painted her to be."

"I simply reported the facts."

His brother stood there breathing hard for a minute before saying, "Did I mention that you're an idiot?"

"It was implied," Lock murmured, grateful that Mike hadn't lost his temper. He liked to be in control, both of himself and a situation.

"Let me state it for the record. Going to bed with the subject of an investigation is about as lame-brained as it gets."

"*Former* subject of an investigation," Lock said.

After a pause, Mike asked, "You going out for dinner?"

"A burger sounds good."

"There's a new health food place on the boulevard," he countered.

Lock had forgotten his brother's fitness kick. "Okay. Give me half an hour to finish a few things."

"Deal."

At the computer, Lock made notes about his meeting with Phil and added reminders on his calendar to check on Kelli. It felt odd, going about his business as if his entire world hadn't shifted on its axis.

Whether he ever saw the baby or held it in his arms, a child descended from him was going to grow up and become…what? How would it feel about being relinquished for adoption? Surely it would spin scenarios about its birth parents, about what kind of people they were and why they'd bowed out of its life.

Not it. He or she. Lock stared down at the photo of Kelli DiDonato, tangled brown hair falling across her shoulder as she bent to light a cigarette. He didn't want his son or daughter to grow up neglected.

Is this how my birth mother felt about giving me up—torn and uncertain? Maybe it was time to find out the truth. Besides, this child deserved a medical history.

Lock accessed the adoption site. Up came the option of forwarding an email address.

If he did locate his mother, he wondered how she'd react to the news that she was about to become a grandparent. And that he planned to give up that baby, just as she'd given him up.

He didn't have to tell her, Lock reminded himself. Before he could raise further objections, he checked the Send My Info box and clicked Apply.

Too late to change his mind. For good or ill, he'd cast his ballot with fate.

Chapter Eight

What was it about shopping that helped to soothe the troubled soul? Erica asked herself as she prowled the narrow aisles of A Memorable Décor. The same principle apparently worked for men, too, since her ex-husband used to disappear for hours into electronics stores. But she didn't want to think about him.

Or about Lock and his ridiculous delays. What did the man fantasize was going to happen? If he had any selfish idea about playing daddy on weekends while Erica turned into Supermom, he'd better to get over that fast.

Their encounter had left her so rattled that only a trip to her favorite store seemed likely to dispel the mood. Erica gazed around, enjoying the array of cabinets, chairs and tables, some old, some reproductions. On one wall hung a lovely needlepoint rug, its maroon expanse enlivened by fanciful flowers.

She studied a glass-topped cocktail tray that might fit into her living room. The price ran higher than the amount on her gift certificate, but it would be handy to have a place for decanters, bottles and glasses when she entertained.

Not that she did much of that. But one of these days she might.

You wouldn't want something this delicate around a small child.

Oh, for Pete's sake.

What about an upholstered ottoman with carved legs? Erica would enjoy propping up her feet while reading a novel. She could replace the worn fabric with something brighter.

Parents don't have time to indulge in reading novels.

Maybe not, she mentally snapped, in response to the inner voice that sounded vaguely like her mother's. But pregnant women did.

Her mother. Ouch. Since learning of her pregnancy this afternoon, Erica hadn't had a chance to consider how Bernadette "Bibi" Benford might react. Although she lived on the East Coast, there'd be no way to keep her in the dark for the next eight months.

After Erica's father died of an aneurysm a few years earlier, Bibi had moved into her fraternal twin sister's house in the Boston suburb of Brookline. A year later, following a divorce, their younger sister, Lily, had joined Bibi and Mimi. Pooling their resources, the three sisters took cruises and seemed to enjoy their lives. In their mid-to late fifties, they all looked considerably younger, thanks to good genes and Botox.

Mimi and Lily had grandchildren, and Bibi frequently hinted that she'd love some of her own. No doubt she'd give plenty of reasons why Erica ought to take on twenty years of hard labor. It was not a conversation she looked forward to.

"Beautiful, isn't it?" A female voice broke into her thoughts.

"Sorry?" Erica realized she was standing in front of an oak crib with butterflies carved into the headboard.

Beside her, she recognized the cheerful, creased face of Renée Green.

"It's the kind of heirloom that gets handed down from generation to generation," said the kindly hospital volunteer.

There aren't going to be any generations in my family, Erica thought with a pang. Well, unless she counted her cousins' children, but she scarcely knew them.

"I wasn't considering buying it. Just lost in thought." Not wanting to seem abrupt, she added, "Do you have children?"

The older woman took a moment to answer. "Not really...no."

This must be a sensitive topic. Perhaps the lady had stepchildren she didn't get along with, or maybe she'd lost a child. "You weren't kidding when you said you love this store," Erica said to change the subject. "I've never seen anyone else I know here."

"Spending your gift certificate?" Renée asked.

"That's the idea." Usually this was the point at which Erica excused herself, but she missed chatting with friends. "Bailey's very considerate, isn't she? Left to his own devices, I'm sure Dr. T would have forgotten my birthday entirely. Or given me a box of chocolates."

"And the rest of the staff would eat the best pieces." Renée chuckled. "That's how it worked at my old office, anyway."

They strolled the aisles, examining items that might fit Erica's decor. "You like butterflies," Renée observed as they lingered in front of a love seat printed with the pretty creatures. "I noticed the cushions Dr. Denny gave you."

"They're my favorite. By the way, he doesn't like being called Doctor. He has a Ph.D., not an M.D. and he's always afraid someone will expect him to know CPR," Erica said automatically. "Oh, sorry. I've worked with him for so long, I've memorized his spiel."

"He's cute. I'm sure before he was married, women asked him to perform CPR all the time."

Erica laughed. "I'm sure they tried, but they didn't get far. His first wife was a real drama queen, and after the divorce, he spent all his spare time raising their little girl."

They skirted a young couple examining a lacquered chest. "I forget how well you know the Boston staff members," Renée said. "It's just that you… This isn't meant as criticism, but you've kept apart since you arrived."

Might as well explain, since the topic was sure to arise. "I went through a difficult divorce recently. Conversations always turn personal, and then people gossip. You've seen that, I'm sure."

Renée touched her arm lightly. "People do like to talk, but at Safe Harbor, they're sympathetic, once you get to know them."

"Coming into a new environment like this, well, it's a bit intimidating." Erica had never admitted that to anyone before. "I suppose I'm more comfortable sticking close to my old team."

"They obviously feel close to you," Renée responded. "I haven't seen Dr. Tartikoff celebrate anyone else's birthday. Bailey says you're indispensable."

She'd have to be replaced at least temporarily when pregnancy made it difficult to stand for hours, Erica thought. "No one's indispensable. I wasn't sure at first that I'd be able to move to California, but that didn't stop Owen from taking the new position. Nor should it have."

She was talking too much. In another minute, she'd start chatting about her pregnancy, and Erica would hate for that to get around the hospital any sooner than necessary.

"You'll find your niche at Safe Harbor," Renée went on. "Everyone respects you, and I think they'd welcome the chance to get closer. When you're ready, you'll have plenty of friends."

"I'm not much of a social animal. But thanks."

A stylishly dressed saleswoman approached. "Can I help you?"

"I'm afraid I haven't fallen in love with anything yet." Although Erica felt an itch to make a purchase, none of the pieces screamed, *Take me home!* She preferred to save her gift certificate for a special item. Since the store received deliveries several times a week, she shouldn't have to wait long.

"Let me know if you have any questions. I'm happy to answer them."

After the woman moved off, Renée said, "My house is so crowded, I can't buy anything until I give away the items I never use. Now that I think of it, I have a tea set with butterflies that would suit you better than me. Why don't you come over and take a look?"

It was a generous offer. But gifts meant obligations. While Erica liked Renée, she wasn't ready for a friendship that went beyond the casual.

"That's very kind, but I'm tired tonight. Let's get together another time." She hoped she didn't come across as unfriendly.

Renée took the response in stride. "When you're in the mood, let me know." She jotted an address and phone number on a pad. "Here's my information. I don't live far from here."

"Thanks. If you decide you'd rather keep your china, I'll understand," Erica said. "We can just have tea."

"Either way is fine with me."

A few minutes later, as Erica was getting into her car,

it occurred to her that she hadn't thought about Lock for at least half an hour. For that, among other things, she was grateful to Renée.

BY FRIDAY, LOCK knew he should have signed the paper. He'd had plenty of time since Tuesday to think about it, and logic kept dictating that he agree to Erica's choice. If he was smart, he'd mail the document to her and be done with it.

His gut refused to let him. Maybe it was the lingering uncertainty about his own origins and why his birth mother had decided to entrust him to the Vaughns. Until he knew that, he wouldn't feel ready to part with this child forever.

On Wednesday morning, he'd received a response from one of the three women who fit his parameters. Turned out she and her husband had given up the baby when they were teenagers, years before they finally married. The picture she'd sent of herself, her husband, their three children and five grandkids showed a handsome Hispanic family that bore no physical resemblance to Lock. He'd responded with his thanks and an explanation about his blond, blue-eyed coloring.

Woman number two had emailed to say that she'd already located her birth son, as confirmed by a DNA test. She apologized for not removing her information from the website.

And behind door number three we have...the mystery lady.

She hadn't contacted him. Even if she did, there was no guarantee she would turn out to be Lock's biomom, as he'd started to think of her. She might be just another dead end.

Still, she'd posted her information. Now that he'd responded, didn't she at least owe him the courtesy of a reply?

There were additional adoptee sites Lock could check, plus public records, but he disliked homing in on a birth mother who didn't want be found. Besides, he'd promised Erica to resolve this situation by Friday.

That afternoon, Lock swung by the middle school as classes were letting out. No sign of Kelli, but then, he hadn't expected to see her in the open. At a nearby pharmacy where the kids sometimes shopped for, or stole, makeup and other personal items, he bought breath mints and made a quick survey of the aisles. Not here, either.

In the parking lot, Lock saw a young mother remove a baby from a car seat and lift him in the air, chirping lovingly. The little fellow giggled in delight. What a cute kid.

Just get this over with and quit torturing yourself.

A block away, he recognized a couple of Kelli's teen-age buddies downing fries at an open-air table in front of a hamburger joint. The girl hadn't joined them this afternoon. Good.

Next stop: the medical center.

Situated on high ground about a mile inland from the beach, the facility had been known as Safe Harbor Community Hospital when Lock was growing up. An out-of-state hospital corporation had bought it a few years back and remodeled it into a center for women and children, adding further upgrades before launching a world-class fertility program last year. Lock subscribed online to the *Orange County Register,* so even while living in Arizona he'd kept current about his home county.

He drove past the six-story buildings and parked. From his briefcase, he extracted the file folder. Despite Mike's warning, he had no fear that signing it would make him liable for anything. Either he was the dad or he wasn't.

Thanks to modern science, paternity was easily determined.

Besides, he didn't believe there was another man in the picture. If there were, Lock would have spotted him while investigating Erica. Nope, he was the guy. *So sign the damn thing.*

Instead, he returned it to his briefcase and went into the lobby. At the front desk, he asked the receptionist to page Erica Benford.

"She's in a meeting," the woman said promptly.

"She's expecting me." If she wasn't available, surely she'd have called. He'd given her his cell number.

"The time of the staff meeting was changed," the receptionist explained. "We're not supposed to page anyone unless it's urgent."

Lock didn't appreciate having to wait. Maybe he should leave and let Erica find *him.* But he had only this stranger's word for the fact that she was unavailable.

And he'd been looking forward to seeing Erica. Usually, with the women he'd dated, he instinctively pulled away when the relationship grew too intimate. He'd never before met a woman who withdrew further and faster than he did.

"Sherlock!" A hale, masculine voice yanked him from his thoughts. "Good to see you." Alec Denny, his shaggy brown hair slanting across his forehead, thrust out his hand, and they shook. "What brings you to the hospital, or is it some hush-hush detective business? Patty's always telling me I'm too nosy."

Lock hoped his colleague's outgoing husband could help. "I just need a moment with Erica Benford. We have an appointment, but I hear she's in a staff meeting."

"I'm on my way there now. Dr. Tartikoff's making an

announcement. Come on. You can catch Erica when it's over."

"It isn't restricted to staff?"

"Whatever he plans to say, there'll be a press release for the media, so it won't be a secret for long." The embryologist started across the lobby, and Lock swung into step beside him.

He was glad to take action, and appreciated the opportunity to learn more about Erica's boss. Although he'd seen Dr. Tartikoff's photo in the paper, it didn't give much sense of the man's personality.

They passed a glass-fronted gift shop filled with balloons, stuffed animals and flowers, and traversed a corridor. Rounding a corner, they reached a set of double doors just as a pretty, dark-haired woman was pulling them shut.

"Sorry. Lost track of time," Alec told her. "Lock, this is our public relations director, Jennifer Martin. Jen, Detective Sherlock Vaughn."

Jennifer cast a questioning glance at Lock, but didn't challenge his admittance. She nodded a greeting before closing them inside.

The wood-paneled auditorium buzzed with conversation, its steeply raked seats packed with men and women in scrubs, white coats and pastel nursing outfits. Lock scanned for Erica, but before he could locate her, an auburn-haired man strode onto the stage below. From his confident movements to his faintly amused air as he surveyed the audience, there was no doubt he must be the famous Dr. T.

This was the guy who dominated Erica's life, Lock mused. Charisma and power flowed from the surgeon who, he recalled reading, had been educated at Harvard and Yale. Probably descended from a long line of elite doctors and professors.

"You'd never guess his mother was a housekeeper and his father spent years in a Russian prison camp as a dissident, would you?" murmured Alec, standing beside Lock at the back of the room.

With renewed respect, Lock watched the man raise a hand for silence. Unnecessarily, since the babble dropped off quickly.

"First, let me say that what I'm about to announce has the full blessing of our hospital administration." Dr. T indicated a man in a business suit sitting in the front row. All Lock could see of him was thick black hair and shoulders worthy of a quarterback. "So if you have any complaints, see Dr. Rayburn."

A ripple of laughter ran through the room. Next to Lock, Alec grinned, obviously enjoying the show.

"Now that I've covered my gluteus maximus, here's the deal." The surgeon paused for effect. "Oh, wait. Do we have some unexpected visitors with a point to make? Let's bring them out."

A lusty wail from the wings was followed by the creak of a baby carriage. Out rolled a double stroller pushed by a pretty, brown-haired woman. Bailey, Dr. T's wife. Lock had met her when she'd dropped by the agency after having lunch with Patty.

The doctor bent to pick up a little, curly-haired girl in a pink romper. Riding high on her daddy's shoulder, she stared at the crowd wide-eyed, then buried her face in his neck. A ripple of "Aws" ran through the audience.

"Reminds me of my Fiona when she was a baby," Alec said fondly.

Small arms encircled her father's neck as if she were clinging on for dear life. Such trust. Lock could almost feel the warmth of her tiny body.

"Believe it or not, there's a reason I brought the twins

on stage, other than the fact that I dote on them," Dr. T continued. "In the fertility program, we get excited about the latest technologies, all those fascinating gadgets and hormones and medications. We tend to lose sight of what it's all about—helping patients have babies. Lots of babies. The more the merrier, or should I say messier? But that's my wife's department."

Lock didn't join in the chuckles. He was too caught up staring at the little girl, who'd summoned the nerve to raise her head again and peer out at the audience.

He could have sworn she was staring directly at him across the room. Sending him a message.

Suddenly Lock understood what he had to do. And it didn't involve signing that waiver.

Chapter Nine

Although she'd been looking forward to Dr. T's announcement, Erica found her nerves stretched tight. First, due to an emergency surgery, the meeting had been postponed from one until three, which should have left plenty of time to make her appointment with Lock. Then the operation ran longer than expected, and while Owen had been able to inform the administration of the delay, Erica could hardly excuse herself from the O.R. to make a personal call.

When she'd tried to reach Lock a few minutes ago, his phone had gone to voice mail. She hoped he would find her message asking him to drop off the waiver. That would be best, anyway.

She couldn't miss the staff meeting, which was mandatory for all personnel not immediately required for patient care. Not only that, but Erica knew her presence mattered to Dr. T. Although he hadn't confided the final details, she'd played a key role in helping him toss around ideas and refine his plans. She was honored to be part of his core team.

"I've been bugging a lot of you over the past few weeks," Owen continued, adjusting his squirming daughter against his shoulder. "You've raised some interesting ideas and shot down others. So in a sense, what I'm about to reveal is a group effort. Like it or not, you're all a part of it."

They were? Erica understood the importance of building teamwork across the entire hospital, but it hadn't occurred to her that so many people were providing input. Suddenly she didn't feel so special, and that hurt more than it should have.

This wasn't her family. It was her work environment. Why did that thought bother her so much?

"We're going to hold a contest that will last for nine months. That's symbolic, as I'm sure you've all figured out." Owen's chuckle made it clear he enjoyed the spotlight. "Our goal is to encourage all of you to make full use of the latest techniques to help our patients. To that end, our medical center management has promised to donate one hundred thousand dollars..." He paused to let the surprised murmur die. "That's one hundred thousand big ones, to the favorite charity of the doctor who achieves the highest pregnancy rate among his or her fertility patients."

No one spoke. Probably, like Erica, they were trying to process what they'd just learned. It came as a shock to her, too. She hadn't heard even the tiniest hint that there might be such a large prize involved.

"We will not count naturally occurring pregnancies among nonfertility patients," Owen added. *Too bad Paige can't count me,* Erica reflected.

"Also, I encourage physicians to choose a charity in consultation with their nurses and other staff. We're all in this together. As for the clock, it starts ticking now, and we'll announce the winner in December. Any questions?"

The first hand that shot up belonged to Dr. Samantha Forrest. "Do pediatricians count?"

"You planning to encourage pregnancies among your little patients?" Owen returned wryly.

The blonde specialist smiled. "I didn't mean it that way. But as most of you know, I established the Edward Serra Memorial Clinic a few years ago to counsel teen moms, abused women and families in crisis. We've been underfunded ever since, and we're operating out of bare-bones quarters at the city's community center. I hope doctors will keep us in mind when they make their choice."

Zack Sargent got to his feet. "If we're lobbying for causes, I hope my fellow OBs will consider setting up a fund to aid patients who lack insurance coverage for fertility treatment. I'm sure we all hate seeing women leave for economic reasons."

More voices joined in, some siding with Samantha or Zack, others offering other choices. Dr. T beamed. "Competition is all to the good."

"Are you going to compete?" Rod Vintner asked him.

"Sure. I hope to raise the stakes for everyone. And the money *does* go to charity."

Paige Brennan stood and waved for attention. With her dramatic red hair and imposing height, she drew all eyes. "While I'm new on staff and technically just filling in for Nora, I'd like to offer another viewpoint."

"By all means," Owen exclaimed. When little Julie, who'd been muttering unhappily, let out a squawk, he handed her to his wife.

"I came here because I love being part of this exciting program," Paige said, "but I think it's important not to pressure patients to go full speed ahead if it doesn't suit their wishes or beliefs. I have couples who prefer a low-tech approach, and sometimes that works."

"All pregnancies among fertility patients count, regardless of which technique was or wasn't used," Dr. T replied. "Anyone else?"

He hadn't acknowledged Paige's point, Erica thought as the obstetrician folded her tall frame back into her seat. And it had taken courage to speak out that way. Well, they all knew Dr. T could be single-minded in pursuit of his goals.

No one else cared to comment. "Go forth and multiply," Owen concluded. "Just keep it civil, folks. The public will be watching. I broke the news here first, but I'll be repeating this information at a press conference later."

As she arose, Erica wondered where she'd donate the money if it were up to her. While a hundred thousand dollars might not be a lot by research standards, it could accomplish a great deal in any of the programs mentioned. But she doubted Dr. T would put much store in her opinion if he won.

She'd better hurry and call Lock, she thought as she made her way up the aisle in a throng of coworkers. But when she reached the top, she saw him standing to one side, waiting for her.

A zone of calm seemed to surround him. His self-assured stance warned people not to push too close, and they didn't.

"I tried to reach you," she said as she joined him. "I'm sorry you had to wait."

"No problem." He didn't explain how he'd slipped into the meeting. "That was quite a show. Dr. Tartikoff has a striking presence."

As they exited the auditorium, Erica regarded her visitor suspiciously. Why was he trying to get on her good side? "The cafeteria's usually half-empty at this hour. We could talk there."

"Fine with me." Cupping her elbow, Lock steered her out of the path of a woman in a wheelchair.

As they headed along the hallway, Erica noticed several people studying the two of them speculatively. Darned if that didn't include Ned Norwalk. She was trying hard to like the blond nurse, especially since they both assisted the same physician, but his nosiness irritated her.

The cafeteria would be too public. Come to think of it, the entire hospital teemed with busybodies with busy ears. Then Erica got an idea. "This way." Turning, she opened a door marked Fertility Support Services.

"Glad you know your way around," Lock said.

"I'm learning."

The receptionist was tied up on the phone, Erica saw. Several other staff members, including the program's financial counselor and patient liaison, were away from their desks, probably due to the meeting. That left several unmarked offices reserved for the yet-to-arrive heads of the egg donor program and the men's fertility program.

She was glad to find one of the doors unlocked. Flicking on the light, she ushered Lock into a bare office save for a desk and a swivel chair.

He cocked an eyebrow. "And I thought my office was underdecorated."

"This isn't mine. It's unoccupied. Well?" Erica gestured at his briefcase.

He indicated the swivel chair. "Sit. Please."

Why? This ought to be a quick meeting. But her legs ached from standing during surgery, and maternal hormones were sapping what energy remained. Besides, Tony had urged her to treat the father with respect.

Lips pressed tight, Erica obeyed.

"I've been giving this a lot of thought." Lock clasped his hands behind his back, like a soldier at ease. "The thing is…I've decided…" He stopped. "No, that's not right."

"What are you trying to say?" Erica asked impatiently.

"I'm going to keep the baby. I'll raise it myself."

She waited for an explanation or—her preference— a "just kidding." For a wild moment, she wondered if it might be April Fool's Day. No, not for another week. The only things she heard were a phone ringing in the outer office and the receptionist's voice answering. Nothing from Lock.

Despite her resolve to be polite, Erica blurted, "You're an idiot."

"My brother agrees with you," Lock said calmly.

"You've discussed this with him?"

"Not about keeping the baby," he said. "I didn't realize that's what I wanted to do until a few minutes ago."

He couldn't be serious, yet apparently he was. "What brought you to this astounding conclusion?"

The planes of Lock's face softened. When his mouth curved tenderly, Erica remembered with a pang how he'd gazed at her on the night they'd made love.

Which is how we got into this mess.

Lock spoke affectionately. "That little girl on the stage was so… It was as if…I fell in love with her. Knowing that you're carrying our baby…becoming a daddy…well, it's the most wonderful thing that's ever happened to me. I can't give that up."

The devotion on his face sent an intense yearning through Erica. For an instant she wondered what it would be like to create a family with Lock and the baby. To have a home instead of feeling like a perpetual outsider.

But he hadn't offered her that. Besides, even if things went well for a while, one day it would evaporate like the fragrance of a home-cooked meal after you opened a window. She'd be left with another ruined relationship and a broken heart. Plus, this time, a needy child she wasn't prepared to raise.

"You're only thinking of yourself," she told him. "This isn't a puppy you can adopt on impulse and find a new home for when you get tired of it. Not that anyone should do that to an animal, but you of all people should understand how cruel it is to a child."

Lock leaned on the edge of the desk, only a couple of feet away. Did he have to smell so alluringly masculine? "I understand your doubts, especially given my lack of experience with babies, but my foster mom can advise me on that. I'll hire help while I'm working, of course."

The hospital's day-care center took infants, Erica remembered. But she didn't want to make this easier for him. "You think I'll come around, don't you? That I'll end up taking responsibility for this child."

"Not at all."

"You say that, but there's an underlying assumption that you'll have backup, and guess who's going to be nominated?" The prospect of being pressured into such a life-altering role infuriated her. "I'll give you credit for good intentions. I'm sure you have a fantasy about how an adoring baby will make up for your lost childhood."

"You don't know me very well." Lock regarded her levelly. "I'm not big on fantasizing."

"You have no idea what it means to assume twenty-four-hour-a-day responsibility for another person," Erica retorted. "This isn't a TV show about a bumbling daddy who magically makes everything work out."

He was nodding, which gave her a glimmer of hope, until he said, "I grant you, I'm a novice. But women cope with this kind of situation all the time. That doesn't mean it's easy, but if they can do it, so can I."

If he wasn't nearly twice her size, she'd have been tempted to shake some sense into him. Or, Erica conceded reluctantly, she might simply be experiencing a desire to touch him. Angry as he made her, there was something appealing about seeing fatherly instincts surface in such a rough-and-tumble guy.

She rejected her impulse. Responding to him on anything other than a rational level would make her as foolish as he was.

"I may not be up for a mother of the year award, but I do feel an obligation to ensure this baby finds the right home," she responded tautly. "You are in no way qualified. Go see a therapist and find out what's really going on inside you, but first please sign that paper."

He spread his hands apologetically. "Your response is understandable. I sprang this on you without warning."

"It may be understandable, but it's also correct," Erica declared. "As you just admitted, you reached this decision without thinking it through. You saw a cute baby and your heart went pitty-pat. How long do you suppose that emotion is going to last? I give you a couple of sleepless nights and a few missed appointments while you rush a sick infant to the doctor."

He folded his arms, which made her aware that she was doing the exact same thing. *We're a matched pair of bull-dogs.* Under other circumstances, she might have found that observation amusing.

"Let's take a day to think about it," Lock said. "I'll come by your place tomorrow around six. Bringing groceries. I'll cook, too. Then we can discuss this with clearer perspective."

On the verge of objecting, Erica realized she had little choice. Although she quailed at the notion of his visiting her apartment again, she couldn't force him to waive his rights, and since he roomed with his brother, they could hardly meet at his place. Going anywhere public, they'd risk being seen by coworkers. It was surprising how often Erica ran into people she recognized at the supermarket or, like the other day, even the antiques store. Much as she appreciated the small-town atmosphere of Safe Harbor, she wasn't thrilled about the lack of privacy.

"Since you aren't arguing, I'll take that as a yes." Lock slid off the desk and opened the door.

Erica's fists tightened. She wanted to get this over with now. To have the decision made, to know that after November, she'd be a free woman. No lingering ties to Lock, no hearing about the baby from mutual acquaintances, and no likelihood of running into them and being forced to see her child growing up without her.

Too late. From the outer office, the receptionist was staring inquisitively in their direction.

"Fine," Erica snapped. "Six o'clock. Bring the paper to sign."

"We'll talk." With a maddeningly pleasant smile, Lock left the suite. The receptionist's admiring glance followed him, further annoying Erica.

Making love with him had been a wonderful experience. Why couldn't they have had a chance to enjoy spending time together free of confrontations and disputes? Instead, the damn condom had broken, and now here they were with a child's future at stake. Not to mention their own futures.

Erica wished she'd arranged to meet him today away from the hospital, where he wouldn't have seen that adorable baby girl. Even Erica had itched to pick up little Julie and cuddle her when she'd started fussing. But unlike Lock, Erica had a good notion from babysitting her cousins just how quickly a cranky baby could exhaust you.

En route to the nurses' locker room, she continued fuming. As she'd said, a baby wasn't a toy. Dr. T had the privilege of handing the restless tyke over to his wife. While Bailey was technically on leave from her nursing job, she'd set no date for returning, and obviously reveled in motherhood. Besides, the couple was madly in love. In every way, parenthood suited them.

Neither Erica nor Lock fit that picture. As for his sudden fixation on fatherhood, Erica felt certain a therapist would say he was compensating for his deprived childhood and seeking to relive it through his son or daughter. She had to be an advocate for this child's right to a stable, loving home, preferably with two parents. *Parents a lot better than him or me,* she added silently as she changed to street clothes and retrieved her purse.

Emerging into a hallway, she nearly collided with a volunteer carrying a vase of flowers. "Oh!" As the woman clutched the vase to keep from dropping it, Erica recognized Renée. "I'm so sorry!" they both said.

When the older woman stood there hugging the vase and breathing hard instead of moving on, Erica added, "Are you all right?"

"I should watch where I'm going," she said, her voice trembling.

Erica didn't bother to argue, although she felt equally at fault. "You seem upset. What is it?"

For a suspended moment, she thought Renée might burst into tears. Then the volunteer said, "It's nothing for you to worry about."

Much as she longed for solitude to mull over Lock's unreasonable demand, Erica couldn't ignore such distress. "Do you need to talk?"

Renée's shoulders sagged. "I hate to dump my problems on you, especially since I brought them on myself."

"Dump away."

"I can't right now. I have a lot to do."

Moving aside for an aide pushing a gurney, Erica asked, "When would be a good time to talk?"

"Could you come by my place tonight?" Renée said. "I'd appreciate a sympathetic ear."

"Absolutely." Erica felt honored that the older woman was willing to confide in her.

"I gave you my address, right?"

"Got it." She'd saved the paper Renée had given her. "Say around seven?"

"Perfect."

With a faint smile, the volunteer whisked the vase toward the patient rooms. Although Erica had offered sympathy impulsively, she discovered that she looked forward to spending the evening with her new friend. Not only would it feel good to help someone, but for once, she'd rather not be left alone with her thoughts.

Otherwise, she might spend the entire time stewing over how to defend against Lock's arguments. He could be very persuasive, she had no doubt. But she was determined to stand her ground.

For the child's sake, as well as her own.

Chapter Ten

To compensate for taking personal time off on Friday afternoon, Lock stayed late at the office, researching the case of a runaway husband. There'd been no indications of foul play or suicide in the disappearance two days ago of forty-two-year-old Josiah Eckert, a self-employed handyman. Apparently he'd grown tired of money troubles and bickering with his wife, but that was no excuse for abandoning her and his two stepchildren.

"The real problem is that he's addicted to video games," his frazzled wife had told Lock when he'd visited her house that morning. Resting her feet on an ottoman—she'd explained they hurt from her waitress job—she'd kept busy folding a basket of sheets and towels as they talked. "He's probably holed up in a motel room, glued to a computer screen, but I'm worried about him. Although the police took a report, it doesn't seem like much of a priority for them."

Lock found no activity on the man's credit card. However, according to Mrs. Eckert, her husband had withdrawn five thousand dollars they'd banked for emergencies. Presumably he could stay hidden for a while.

The guy wasn't answering his cell and hadn't contacted any friends. Lock had canvassed the neighbors without luck, and the laptop that held the guy's client list had walked out the door with him. However, Mr. Eckert's haphazard record keeping system might prove his undoing. He'd used copies of old receipts as bookmarks in his stack of girlie magazines, and several had yielded addresses that led to phone numbers. This evening, Lock made half a dozen calls. He received two out-of-service recordings, left messages on three voice mail accounts, and talked to one hard-of-hearing fellow who kept shouting, "What? Who?" until Lock gave up.

He would try again tomorrow. Sooner or later, he'd find Josiah Eckert, or the guy might return on his own. Speaking of finding people... Lock checked his email. Still no word from his possible birth mother. The website should have notified her a few days ago. What was delaying her response, or would there ever be one?

Surely she owed him the courtesy of an answer, so he could at least cross her off his list. And if she actually was his mother, she owed him a lot more than that.

Finally finished with the day's work, Lock drove home. The single-story house he and Mike rented lay on the east side of town, between homes brightened by rose arbors and striped awnings. While the landlord had spruced up the house with new paint, the aging roof had sprung a leak during the recent rains and required emergency patching. As for the lawn and shrubs, they fell into the category of barely adequate.

Lock wanted his kid to grow up in a house he or she could be proud of. Funny, he'd never cared about things like that before.

As he stepped inside, he registered the loud whine of engines accompanied by male voices calling, "Pick it up!" and "Whew! Close one."

He'd once mentioned to a date that guys liked to watch videos of motorcycle racing, and she'd regarded him as if the top of his head had swung open to reveal a nest of snakes. Must be a guy thing.

Sure enough, his brother and a few pals from the police department were sprawled in the living room, beers in hand and feet propped on the coffee table, while bikes roared across the TV screen.

After a wave of acknowledgment, Lock went to pull on some old jeans and a T-shirt. Standing in the middle of his bedroom with its much-pierced dartboard, he realized it wasn't just the exterior that bothered him.

Bunch of beer-drinking guys in the front room. Pool table in the den. Motorcycle videos, a treadmill in Mike's room that creaked and thumped, darts scattered across Lock's bureau and onto the floor. How was an infant going to fit in?

Lock studied the room. Once he cleaned up the darts, he could put a crib by the window. Sharing a room wasn't ideal, but it meant he'd be available whenever the baby needed him. And when it was older, he'd rent a place with an extra bedroom.

He didn't know how to change a diaper, what type of formula to buy or at what age a baby started eating solid food. But he could learn.

While it was true that his foster mom should be a font of good advice, it was too bad she and his foster dad planned to retire soon and tour the country in their RV. As for Mike, he wasn't going to like having a pair of lusty newborn lungs sharing the house.

Am I going off half-cocked? Logically, Lock had to consider the possibility that Erica was right, no matter what his heart told him.

"Yo, Sherlock!" Mike shouted from the other end of the house. "We're ordering pizza. You in?"

"You bet!" Rousing himself from his reverie, Lock hurried to the kitchen.

Three faces greeted him. "You know Hank and Steven, right?" Mike asked.

"Sure." Tall and lean with dark hair silvering around the edges, Steven was the detective lieutenant at Mike's old bureau. Hank, whose eyes, one blue and one brown, gave him a disconcerting gaze, worked crimes against property.

"You want pepperoni, right?" Hank asked.

"Veggie," Mike corrected.

"Here's a wildly extravagant idea. Let's order both," Steven said.

"Whatever." Lock would eat almost anything you could slap on a pizza. Well, not crazy about anchovies.

"And how about some of those deep-fried dessert things with icing?" the lieutenant asked. "My daughter has a fit if I bring sweets into the house, so I'm sugar-deprived. She's on a perpetual diet. I don't think it's an eating disorder, but I'm keeping watch."

Lock recalled Patty mentioning that Steven, a widower, had recently returned from family leave to care for his daughter after a traffic accident. "She's recovered from her injuries?"

"Aside from a few scars and a slight limp, she's perfect." The guy narrowed his eyes at Mike. "Are you going to make that call or do I have to make it for you?"

"Hold your horses." Mike pressed a button. Pizza on speed dial.

"Remember the pepperoni," Hank interjected. "None of that sissy health food for me."

"Veggie pizza is not health food," Mike corrected.

"Says you." Hank wandered into the attached den and

grimaced at the pool table. "What lame brain didn't rack the balls? That's a crime."

Lock, who couldn't remember whether he was the guilty party, ignored the gibe. He had more important things to think about, such as the fact that before him stood a real live single father. A man with answers.

Revealing his situation was out of the question. It would be unfair to make common gossip of Erica's pregnancy, plus there was no telling how Mike might react. Best to be discreet.

As an opening, Lock asked, "Where's your daughter tonight?"

Steven shuddered. "On a date."

He had been picturing a grade schooler. "How old is she?"

"Fourteen," the lieutenant said. "And for reasons I fail to understand, she refuses to wear a chastity belt."

He thought of Kelli DiDonato smoking after school. "How do you keep a lid on things? I get the idea teenagers listen to their friends more than their parents."

Still on the phone, Mike slanted a puzzled glance in his direction.

"I set rules," the lieutenant replied. "Before a date, I meet the guy *and* his parents, and one of the parents has to do the driving. Tonight I dropped the kids off at the movies, and the boy's mother is picking them up."

That sounded reasonable. "She doesn't sneak out?" Quickly, Lock explained, "One of my clients is having problems with his niece."

"I'm frank with her about the dangers out there, and Layla's mature for her age. She's been through a lot." After tossing his beer can into a recycling container, Steven took a diet soda from the fridge. "My wife died when my daughter was eight. Then last year a truck driver plowed into the school bus and put her in the hospital for weeks. She had to be homeschooled for months and relied on me to drive her to therapy. Sometimes a kid requires a full-time parent, and I was the only one on tap."

"Tough financially," Lock sympathized.

"But worth it."

"You sure are fascinated with helping this client," Mike muttered.

"I'm a big-hearted guy," Lock replied, and went to knock a few balls around with Hank.

He spent the rest of the evening trying to act as if everything was normal and ducked into his room after the guests left. Too many thoughts were caroming off each other for him to deal with his brother's third degree.

The strangest part, Lock reflected as he settled back to play a game on his smartphone, was that instead of being put off by the idea of coping with challenges as his son or daughter grew, he found the prospect exhilarating. His brush with death in the bank robbery had raised a lot of issues, not only about where he came from, but about where he was going.

Steven's love for his daughter clearly trumped everything else in his life. How rewarding to watch her develop into a young woman, despite the scary parts.

Lock could picture himself cheering as his son or daughter played sports. Bursting with pride as he or she graduated. *Dad.* Yeah, he wanted that honor. It would be the best reward of all to hear his grown child say to a friend, "My dad was tough on me, but he's the greatest."

Earlier, he'd told Erica he wasn't given to fantasizing. He'd been wrong about that.

But not, Lock concluded, about anything else. Especially the snap decision that was rapidly hardening into an immovable resolution.

THE MOMENT ERICA spotted Renée's fairy-tale cottage, she adored it. After her hostess ushered her inside, she discovered an interior to match, with china cabinets full of figurines, stenciled designs on the walls and upholstery embroidered with flowers.

Cozy as this place was, Renée's jittery manner showed her distress. She bustled about offering to prepare tea or serve cookies, both of which Erica declined. "Please tell me what's on your mind," she said.

"You're sure you won't have tea?"

"I'm fine." Erica settled onto a dainty chair. "It might be easier if you just dive in."

The woman sank into the couch. "Where shall I start?"

"Wherever you like."

Renée inhaled quickly. "I told you once that I didn't have children. That's not entirely true."

"What do you mean?" Erica's interest quickened. She'd expected a confidence regarding finances or health, not this.

"When I was young, I gave up a baby for adoption."

Erica felt a rush of sympathy. "That must have been difficult."

"It was the right decision at the time." Renée chewed her lip before continuing. "Now he's contacted me. Or rather, I heard from the adoption website. I'm afraid I'm not explaining this very well."

"Take your time," Erica said.

The older woman's hands tightened in her lap. "You're very easy to talk to. Well…it's my own fault. After my husband died, a couple of years ago, I posted my name and a little information on this website. I told myself it was so I could answer any questions my son might have, but the truth is, after losing Hubert, I lost my sense of purpose.

For thirty years we'd been everything to each other, and I guess I was hoping to find someone to love."

"Aren't you still?" Erica asked.

Renée shrugged. "I'd almost forgotten about the whole thing, to tell the truth. Once I became involved at the hospital, my feelings of isolation disappeared. Plus I'm sort of an honorary grandmother to Bailey and Dr. T's twins, since they have no living grandparents."

"You said your son contacted you. What did he say?" Erica found the prospect both fascinating and disturbing. What if her son or daughter turned up someday demanding answers?

Renée didn't seem to notice her distraction. "He can't write to me directly. It doesn't work that way. The site sent me his email address and a message indicating he wants to get in touch. That's all."

That didn't seem terribly threatening, especially since the match was apparently based on a small amount of data. "Are you sure he's your son?"

"There's a high probability, in my opinion. The details match—birth date, adoption agency and so forth." Renée swallowed hard. "It's painful to remember those days. I hadn't considered how much this would bring up after thirty-five years."

"You said it was the right decision," Erica reminded her. "But I suppose it's always difficult." Look at how much trouble she was running into with her own situation.

"I was seventeen. My parents were angry with me and in denial about the baby, and I couldn't have raised him on my own." Renée sounded as if she was trying to justify her actions.

"Of course not." Much as Erica disliked prying, her friend needed to get all this off her chest. "What about the father? Didn't he try to help you?"

"He couldn't."

"He was married?"

"Oh, no, nothing like that." Renée blinked hard. "He… I wish—" She broke off.

Erica leaned forward and patted her hand. "You don't have to talk about this."

"Yes, I do." She cleared her throat. "If you don't mind."

"That's why I'm here."

"Vick was two years older than me. Cute and sexy, zooming around in his souped-up car. He'd been in trouble with the law a few times, but nothing serious. He was my parents' worst nightmare, which made him irresistible." A ghost of a smile crossed the woman's face. "Until I met him at a party, I'd always been a Goody Two-shoes."

"He sounds like a rebel." Erica imagined Lock turning out that way if he hadn't found such a loving foster family. "Didn't he stand by you?"

"When I told him about the baby, he was confused. He needed time to think, he said. A few days later, Vick crashed into a light pole while street racing." Tears shimmered against Renée's lashes.

"How awful!"

"While he was in a coma, I visited him every day. When my parents found out I was pregnant, they threatened to send me away, but I defied them for once. Then one day Vick opened his eyes. He couldn't talk yet, but he squeezed my hand. I was so happy, so excited. The next day after school, I rushed to the hospital." Tears slid down her cheeks.

"What happened?"

"He was gone. A blood clot, the doctor said. I'd been counting on us building a life together. But just like that, it was over."

Moving to the couch, Erica slipped an arm around the woman. "How terrible."

"I was sure he'd come around and marry me...." Renée pulled a tissue from her pocket and wiped her eyes. "I was numb with grief. I just turned the baby over to the couple the agency recommended. All these years, I've wondered how my little boy turned out. Well, he's not a little boy anymore."

"I wonder why he's trying to reach you." Perhaps the man needed information about his heredity.

"When I signed up on the website, it seemed harmless." Renée blew her nose. "The past few days, I've been reading birth mothers' blogs. Some of the experiences are wonderful, but other adoptees have unrealistic expectations or unresolved anger. Several women were harassed and one was physically attacked."

"That *is* frightening." Erica didn't like to dwell on such a thought. "You never had other children?"

Her hostess answered calmly. "A few years later, I was lucky enough to marry Hubert. We agreed to stop using birth control for a while, but when nothing happened, we decided not to pursue medical treatments or adoption. Hubert was older than me and fixed in his ways, so maybe it was for the best. I suspect our marriage was happier with just the two of us."

"Good for you. Frankly, I..." Erica hesitated. She'd been about to confess that she didn't want children, either, but that might lead to revealing her pregnancy. And she wasn't ready to share that.

"Oh! I promised you a tea set." Renée sprang from the couch.

"What do you mean?"

"The one with the butterflies."

Erica recalled their conversation at the antiques store. "I'd forgotten about that. There's no need."

"It's right over here." From a sideboard, the woman removed a pale green teapot and placed it lovingly in Erica's hands. "It's perfect for you."

Hand-painted butterflies flew along the surface, their jewel-like wings brilliant. Erica caught her breath. "How lovely!"

"I couldn't resist these darling cups, but they're wrong for my flower theme." She set four small cups and saucers on an end table. Each displayed a different type of butterfly, every one luminous.

"They're too beautiful. I can't accept this." But how could she resist? The painted images were full of life and hope, like a row of bassinets in the hospital nursery.

"I bought them at a crafts fair from the artist himself, on a trip Hubert and I took to Northern California." Renée sat down, her expression eager. "It's such a pleasure to see how much you like them."

"I do!" And then, to Erica's utter dismay, she burst into tears.

Chapter Eleven

"Oh, my dear! I didn't mean to upset you." Renée rushed over, accidentally knocking the end table and setting the china chattering. Both women grabbed the cups and teapot to steady them. "There, there," the older woman said. "I'm so sorry. I've dragged you into my problems without a thought for how they might affect you."

"It's not your fault." Erica couldn't keep her secret any longer. "I'm pregnant. That's why I'm so emotional."

With the china rescued, Renée sank down again. "This wasn't planned, was it?"

She shook her head. "I'm going to place the baby for adoption."

Understanding dawned on her friend's face. "And I've gone poking at your wounds by telling you my problems."

"No, you've just helped me think it through. I'm sure it's the right thing to do. But the father has this crazy notion about keeping the baby." Bits and pieces rushed out, how she'd met the man by chance and made love in a moment of weakness. "Today he saw a cute baby and suddenly decided he's daddy material. He hasn't got a clue what's ahead. And you know what else that means? I'd see my baby around. At the store, at the park, who knows where. It would be torture."

Renée tilted her head sympathetically. "Of course it would. Because your heart is torn in two."

That wasn't what she'd meant. "I'm not in love with him."

"But you're in love with your baby," her friend said, as if stating a fact.

"No! She or he isn't…" *Isn't real to me.* But that implied Erica might change her mind as the pregnancy progressed, and she knew she wouldn't. "The baby belongs with people who're eager for a child. Who'll turn their lives and their home upside down to be good parents."

A picture formed of her beautiful, orderly apartment, her refuge. The table and delicate glassware. The lovingly recovered upholstery. The… What was an image of the crib from the antiques store doing in her thoughts? *It's the kind of heirloom that gets handed down from generation to generation….*

Hot tears streaked her face. How embarrassing. It wasn't as if she'd lost the man she loved the way Renée had. Erica wasn't losing anything.

Was she?

"I suppose I am torn," she admitted reluctantly.

"At least you have a choice, one way or the other," Renée told her. "You're not seventeen, and even if you don't love this man, he's willing to stand by his child. Don't be too hasty. You're making a decision now that will affect the rest of your life."

Reaching for the teapot, Erica idly traced one of the painted butterflies with her finger. She remembered Lock's blazing intensity when he'd told her that becoming a father was the most amazing thing in his life. Would it be so terrible to take a chance on raising a child with him?

It meant assuming a lifelong burden based on trust—

trust in a man she barely knew. A man who could vanish in an instant. Erica refused to be the poor woman left alone to struggle. She knew her own mind a lot better than she knew Lock.

"A part of me may be tempted," she conceded. "But I wasn't cut out for motherhood. Not every woman is."

Renée showed no inclination to argue. "I'm glad you aren't making a snap decision. Now what are you going to do about the father?"

"He's coming over to my apartment tomorrow." By then, Erica had to figure out a way to change his mind. "He's very strong willed."

"Men tend to be like that," Renée said with a trace of irony.

"Him in particular." Strength was one of the qualities Erica most valued in Lock. Sometimes. "I'm afraid that by the time he realizes he's made a mistake, it'll be too late. He'll feel committed and refuse to back down. The poor kid shouldn't have to grow up in that kind of environment."

"Give him a chance to learn more about fatherhood in advance. Babysitting would be a start," her friend advised. "That might help him figure out whether he's ready."

"I wouldn't trust him alone with a baby," Erica declared. "He might hold it upside down while he diapers it. Oh, I don't mean that, but he *is* inexperienced."

"What about you?" Renée asked. "Have you spent much time around small children?"

"My mother made me babysit her sisters' kids. I wouldn't have minded occasionally, but it was practically every weekend." Erica still felt angry about it. Although she'd been allowed to attend important high school functions, she'd missed the chance to hang out with classmates, to share long conversations and sleepovers. She'd had a hard time establishing friendships ever since. "If anyone knows how to warm a bottle or burp a baby, it's me."

"You should teach him." Renée got to her feet and indicated the tea set. "Let me pack these for you."

Erica no longer had the heart to refuse the gift. The butterflies seemed to have been painted especially for her. "This is much too generous. I'll pay you for them."

"Nonsense. Take the tea set and quit beefing about it!"

Erica laughed. "Since you put it that way."

"I'll be right back." Renée scooted into the bedroom and returned with a cardboard box and bubble wrap. They both set to work. "I have an idea! Why don't you and this fellow babysit Dr. Tartikoff's twins? That would be a trial by fire."

"Bailey might enjoy having a night out." Erica *had* heard Owen say his wife didn't like leaving the babies with a stranger, no matter how highly recommended. "I could suggest it. But I'd have to explain why, which means telling Dr. T about my pregnancy."

"How long do you expect to keep it a secret from an obstetrician?" Renée tucked a cup into the box.

"Good point." Erica wrapped the teapot carefully. "Okay, I'll suggest it to the baby's father. If he's willing and Dr. T doesn't agree, I'm sure we can find another parent who'll accept free babysitting."

"Dr. Rayburn and Dr. Forrest have triplets. That would be an even bigger challenge."

Erica filed away that possibility, but she didn't know the hospital administrator and his wife very well. "Thanks. You've been a big help."

"So have you," Renée told her. "I still don't know what I'm going to do about my son, but talking to you was a relief."

Only after Erica had loaded the china into her trunk

and was driving home did she realize that, despite her reservations, she looked forward to tomorrow night. Being around Lock might be fun. So would babysitting together. And once he came to his senses and agreed he wasn't cut out for single fatherhood, she hoped they could be friends.

Friends with benefits. She'd like that.

LOCK HADN'T MEANT to spend an hour on the internet researching recipes for dinner, but he was glad he had, he mused as he selected a package of ground turkey in the supermarket meat section. What was it about Erica that made him want to take care of her? He felt a powerful instinct to make sure she ate properly and stayed safe, and not only due to the pregnancy. Perhaps it was because she seemed brittle, angry and hurt from old injuries, just like he was.

He glanced at his shopping list. Next item: stuffing mix. The recipe called for combining it with ground meat, oregano and a cup of water, dividing the mixture up in a muffin tin, spooning on salsa and baking the mini meat loaves for half an hour at 350 degrees. Topped with cheese and served with corn and a salad, they ought to be tasty, as well as nourishing.

Suncrest Market was busy near dinnertime on a Saturday, its aisles jammed with families, single folks like him and couples. Lock steered his cart around a display of cake mixes and halted in surprise when he recognized the girl ahead of him as Kelli DiDonato. She was staring up adoringly into the face of an unshaved young man with scraggly blond hair. One arm looped around her waist, he reached past her to pluck a box of brownie mix off the shelf.

Lock had seen the fellow before, smoking with Kelli after school, and heard her call him Randy. He'd assumed the youth was in high school, but his T-shirt bore the name of a nearby community college. Did this guy have any idea that the girl was only eleven? Or didn't he care?

Ducking his head to avoid notice, Lock moved to the next aisle. He took out his phone and dialed Phil's number.

Upon learning of the situation, the mechanic said gruffly, "I'll find out if my mother knows what Kelli's doing. Meanwhile, I'm on my way. Call you back."

"I'll keep an eye on her." Lock had nearly finished shopping, anyway. And luckily, this aisle held the stuffing mix.

After dropping it in his cart, he peered into the baking section. Empty. Concerned, he prowled through the store until he spotted the pair in the freezer section. Kelli giggled at something her companion said and snuggled closer. Randy smirked. If that were Lock's daughter, he'd grab her away fast.

"Are you deliberately ignoring me?"

Startled by the female voice, Lock swiveled. Erica stood watching him with wry amusement. "Oh, hi," he said, trying to figure out how to explain the situation.

"You walked right past me. You aren't on duty, are you?" She shifted her cart to make room for another shopper.

"Well, I wasn't, but I am now." He gave a nod toward the pair he'd been observing. "See them? Don't stare. That girl is my client's niece and she's only eleven. I'm on watch until her uncle gets here."

"That guy's way too old for her." Erica kept her voice low and averted her gaze. If Kelli glanced their way, she'd see nothing more than two people chatting. Not that the girl seemed aware that anyone else existed, in the store or possibly in the universe. "I don't suppose you can tell me what's going on with her."

"It's confidential…" Glancing into her cart, Lock noted milk, bread and margarine. "Out of the basics?"

"I figured you might need some of these for cooking," she said. "Should I leave you alone? I'll understand if you're late."

"Actually, talking to you makes me less conspicuous," Lock explained. "Not that I don't enjoy the company."

"Sorry I forgot my trench coat and fedora."

"Let's just pretend we're civilians," he said drily, and stole another glance at his target. To Lock's dismay, Randy and Kelli were kissing, her arms winding around his neck as she pressed against him.

An elderly man shot them an irritated frown. "Get a room," he muttered.

Kelli burst out laughing. After selecting a carton of ice cream from the freezer case, she and Randy sauntered toward the front of the store with their purchases.

Lock indicated the contents of his cart. "Would you mind taking care of this?"

"Not at all. Now, go!" Erica said.

From a nearby shelf, he grabbed a bottle of vinaigrette dressing as an excuse in case he had to stand in line, and strode off. On the way, he skirted mounded displays of fruit, barely halting in time to avoid running into his targets. The couple had paused by a stand of cut flowers to indulge in another passionate kiss.

Through the large front window, Lock searched in vain for Phil's truck. Instead, he noticed a motor home double-parked behind his car. Rotten timing if he had to follow these two.

As Kelli and Randy lingered, Lock made a quick assessment of his options. Running out and shouting "Move!" would make him about as inconspicuous as a

Tyrannosaurus rex in a Starbucks. Besides, he saw Erica's car in the clear.

And she'd wasted no time in hauling their combined stuff to a check stand, where she'd started unloading the items. Lock slipped into place beside her. "Change of plans." He directed her gaze toward the RV. "I'm blocked. Okay if we take your car?"

"Sure. I'm not leaving that kid unprotected."

The younger couple was using a self-serve counter. Anxious to keep up with them, Lock hurried things along by bagging the groceries. "Used to do this in high school," he told the clerk.

"You're good at it," she said. "If you ever need a job, let us know."

"Thanks."

By the time they trailed their quarry outside, a large tow truck was backing toward the RV. That explained why the driver hadn't removed it.

Stopping at a dented compact car, Kelli set their small grocery bag in the trunk. Randy kept putting his hands all over her. "She's eleven?" Erica muttered. "He ought to be arrested."

"He might be." Lock's phone rang. "Yes?"

"She told Mom she was spending the night with a girl-friend." Judging by the background noise, Phil was on the road.

"I'm in the parking lot at Suncrest."

"I'm turning in now."

Sure enough, a pickup with Phil's Garage emblazoned on it was pulling in from the street. "See that tow truck hooking up the RV?" Lock said into the phone. "They're two lanes to the east."

"Got 'em." The pickup rolled toward the oblivious young lovers.

Lock pointed it out to Erica. "The cavalry's arrived."

She clicked her tongue as the truck came to a halt. "Too bad. I was all set for one of those exciting car chases like on TV."

"Don't be too disappointed. It's hard to tail a vehicle in traffic."

Near the dented compact, Phil double-parked and stalked toward the pair. As Kelli's uncle spoke, Randy's demeanor shifted from defiance to dismay. He made no attempt to intervene as Phil hauled his niece to his truck. Though Lock couldn't hear their exchange at this distance, he could read the girl's resentment in her body language.

Too bad his client didn't handle the situation with a bit more tact. While this incident might persuade the grandmother to clamp down harder, she couldn't keep the girl under lock and key twenty-four hours a day. Even if Randy left Kelli alone, it wouldn't take her long to latch on to another exploitive male.

"What does a parent do in that situation?" Lock asked. "You can't force her to follow the rules."

"You're genuinely concerned about her, aren't you?" Erica watched him thoughtfully.

"She's so vulnerable." Unable to explain Kelli's family situation, he had to keep his remarks general. "Children's needs are profound, and kids grow up fast."

"That's why it's better if they have two parents who're dedicated to them." As the pickup rolled away, Erica opened her car door. "But if you really think you're ready to parent on your own, I'll do what I can to get you off to a good start."

"You mean that?" A few lanes over, Lock saw the tow truck roll forward slowly with the RV hooked behind it.

She sighed. "Yes, I mean it. And no, I don't."

"What are you saying?" Lock asked.

In the fading light, her pale hair took on an ethereal quality. "I'm willing to babysit with you, and teach you how to change diapers and bottle-feed. But the truth is, I'm hoping you'll hate every minute of it."

He had to smile at her honesty. "Fair enough. We can discuss this over dinner."

"Meet you at my place," she said.

With a wave, Lock headed for his car. While he had no idea what had changed Erica's mind, it was a start.

A start toward what, he had no idea. But he was more than willing to find out.

Chapter Twelve

The way Lock moved around her kitchen made Erica feel like a giddy teenager struggling to tear her eyes from the ripple of muscles beneath his shirt. When he peeled back his sleeves to wash his hands, the sight of his muscular forearms reminded her of how he'd held himself over her as they'd made love.

Sitting on the far side of the breakfast counter, she realized that she'd missed his sideways grin and his self-assured manner. And seeing the way he cared about that girl at the supermarket had forced her to concede that his desire to keep the baby might prove more than a passing whim. Was it possible that, despite the emotional knocking around he'd received as a child, he'd emerged with true paternal instincts?

The prospect was incredibly sexy.

The best thing about him, she decided, was that he never seemed to be trying to dominate her. He didn't assume that she would take on the role of his kitchen helper, nor had he pressed her further about her babysitting promise. Instead, he'd kept the conversation light and gone to work with a will.

Not that Erica trusted him past a certain point. Sooner or later, guys let you down. Even Dr. T had disappointed her yesterday when he'd relegated her to a role as one in a cast of, well, dozens. But on a scale of one to ten, she was willing to grant Lock a seven for responsibility. Possibly an eight.

He opened the oven, releasing the delicious scent of meat and spices. "Nearly done. I like this recipe. Hope you do, too."

"My mouth's watering." *And not just for dinner.* "You're quite a cook."

"It's a simple meal." Lock set a bowl of salad on the counter. "You can put this on the table if you like."

She transferred the bowl to the table, which she'd set while he worked. "Do you ever lie to women?"

He blinked. "About salad? Never."

Erica returned to her post. "What *do* you lie about?"

"My foster mother told me that there are certain questions a man should never answer truthfully." He put a corn casserole into the microwave oven.

"Which questions?" Erica had never considered what sort of advice a mother might give a son. Bibi's tips about male-female relationships had mainly consisted of ways to build up a man's ego. Once Erica discovered that most men's egos didn't require building up, she'd stopped listening.

"First, 'Does this make me look fat?' The answer is always no."

She chuckled. "Agreed."

"Ditto for, 'Does this make me look old?'"

"Anything else?"

He considered. "'Have you ever loved anyone before?'"

"I thought I did when I got married, but… Was that a question or an example?"

"Both," Lock said.

She felt her cheeks heating. "How about you? Ever been in love?"

"I've had crushes. Not recently."

"What does that mean?"

Lock finished wiping down the counter and moved toward her. The air shimmered between them. "It means that, hopefully, I've matured." He leaned on the counter, his hand inches from hers. It was a strong hand, sprinkled with dark hairs and marked with a small, jagged scar.

She traced the scar with her finger. "What happened here?"

"Fish hook. Camping accident." His voice had a throaty rasp and she saw a quiver run up his arm.

"You're a real man's man, aren't you?"

"Sometimes I'm a woman's man." His gaze flashed with liquid fire.

"I can vouch for that," Erica agreed.

"I'd be happy to prove it to you again."

She swallowed. "Now?"

"Seize the moment." A kitchen timer buzzed, followed a moment later by the microwave. "Hold that thought." Grabbing oven mitts, Lock removed the muffin tin to the stovetop, leaving the casserole in place. "These need to cool and I can reheat the corn."

"This is becoming a habit. Maybe you should stop cooking for me."

"Or we should make love first. But if I have to choose between appetites, I know which one will always win."

So did she. When Lock came around the counter to take her in his arms, Erica felt not the least inclination to resist.

By the time they reached the bedroom, he'd unbuttoned her blouse and she'd helped pull his sweater over his head. "Guess you can skip the protection," she teased.

"Darn, and I just bought a replacement." His mouth

claimed hers, halting any response. But then, she didn't have one.

Erica reveled in the chance to explore Lock at leisure, to touch his powerful shoulders and back. Her passion built as his mouth and tongue inflamed her breasts, trailing down to an area so sensitive she could hardly bear it.

When he lowered her to the bed and joined them with a thrust, pleasure exploded inside her. And there was more—tantalizingly more. Joy rolled through Erica in waves. Lock cried out, thrusting into her again and again, until he sank atop her, breathing hard.

After a moment, he shifted to the side and they lay enveloped in heat. "We should do this more often," Erica murmured.

"I second that motion," Lock said and kissed her.

WHILE HE HADN'T had any specific expectations when he'd invited himself over to cook dinner, Lock supposed that he'd hoped all along they would make love again. Being inside Erica fused the fragments of his soul, resonating beyond the physical.

Always before, at this deepening stage of a relationship, he'd felt an uneasy push-pull between wanting more and hearing the sound of a prison door creaking shut. The closer the woman drew, the more Lock felt driven toward the exit.

Not with Erica. When they showered together, she stroked him plenty, but there was always a hint of distance in her smile. He heard no creaking, saw no dwindling glimmer of light through a fast-closing door. An unfamiliar pang of uncertainty ran through Lock as she dried off and dressed, ran her hand across his chest appreciatively and went out.

She wasn't leaving, just going to the kitchen. Yet with

Erica, he made no assumptions about the future. *She's too much like me.*

He hurried to catch up. "Dinner's my job," Lock told her when he heard the microwave humming.

"Joint effort. Don't go all controlling on me," she warned, tugging back a strand of damp blond hair.

"You hate that in guys as much as I hate it in women," he blurted.

"I hope you don't get any sense I'm trying to run your life," she returned sharply.

"Not at all."

"Good. As far as I'm concerned, you're free to go. Not that I'm trying to get rid of you." She took out a serving platter and began spooning meat loaf out of the muffin pockets.

The remark stung. Lock had always taken it for granted that if he found the "right" relationship, the woman would love him as much as he loved her, or more. "Aren't some people worth holding on to?"

"Didn't you hear me say I'm not trying to get rid of you?" Carrying the platter, Erica moved from the kitchen to the table.

Lock followed with the corn casserole. "That's hardly a ringing endorsement."

"Don't worry," Erica said. "I still have to teach you how to change diapers."

That wasn't enough for him. "You'll need a birth partner. I'd like to do that for you." His foster mother had fulfilled that role for Lourdes while her husband was on a tour of duty with the marines. Lock remembered the two of them discussing how the experience had brought them closer.

Erica took a seat. "Don't remind me of what's ahead. I dread all this."

"Some women find pregnancy and childbirth fulfilling." That was the wrong thing to say, Lock gathered from her skeptical look. "However, I'm not the one who has to go through it."

"Exactly."

"Did you have someone else in mind?" he pressed.

"For what?" She heaped food on her plate.

Was she purposely putting him off? Lock wondered as he sat beside her. "Birthing partner."

"Don't need one. I expect the doctor to knock me out. If someone tries to tell me how to breathe, I'll kick him in the shins. Or somewhere else, since I'll be lying down," she qualified.

To Lock, this was no longer a joking matter. "I'm serious about the offer."

"I'll consider it," Erica replied. "Now are you going to pass the salad or do I have to sit on your lap and reach for it myself?"

He liked that offer. "You're welcome to sit on my lap."

"Just wait till the baby and I weigh three hundred pounds," she threatened. "We'll mash you into the chair."

"I'm looking forward to it," Lock said, only half kidding. Then he passed the salad.

On Sunday, they made love twice. This friends-with-benefits business would be sheer heaven if it weren't for the burning question of what to do about the baby, Erica thought.

She kept remembering Renée's dilemma. How wrenching to give up a baby and then, years later, have to deal with a complete stranger, an adult with possible unresolved issues. But how much worse to see that child around town as he or she was growing up. How could anyone turn a cold shoulder to a sweet little kid who lacked a mother?

And how was Erica going to put a wall between herself and Lock after the baby's birth? The only solution would be to move away. Leave the hospital and Dr. T's team.

Or stay here and help raise the child. Work something out with Father Knows Best. It would be unconventional to give the baby to Lock, yet stay involved. Well, who said she had to live according to convention?

Of course, that assumed she could rely on Lock to keep his end of the bargain. To be a real father, to build his life around the child. To accept Erica as a part-time mom and sometime lover. Yet after this weekend, she was beginning to think that might be possible.

First things first. She'd promised to set up the babysitting gig.

On Monday, Erica managed to get a moment alone with Dr. T in the break room. Talking quickly before anyone else came in, she told him about her pregnancy, the father's wish to raise the child, and their interest in babysitting the twins. "It's kind of a boot camp for an inexperienced dad."

"I'm supposed to trust my kids to a rookie?" He quirked an eyebrow.

"Under my supervision." Erica had thought that was clear.

"It won't be a fun date," Owen warned. "If one twin goes to sleep, the other fusses and wakes up."

"That's the idea," Erica said. "I hope Lock will discover he's not cut out for the daddy business, after all."

Or did she hope that? It had been her intention initially. But such a realization might break Lock's heart. She almost hoped he'd choose to keep the baby.

Almost.

"I'll ask my wife. We'd love to see *South Pacific* at the Orange County Music Center next weekend." Owen jammed his hands into the pockets of his white coat. "You know, I wasn't too keen on being tied down before I learned Bailey was expecting. You might change your mind."

"Let's not go there," Erica warned. In the hallway, she heard footsteps and braced for an interruption. To her relief, no one entered.

Dr. T's cinnamon eyes swept her protectively. "Who is this guy, anyway? How'd you let him knock you up?"

She laughed at his choice of words. "Fine talk from a fertility expert."

"Answer the question."

"He's a detective. His name's Lock Vaughn and he works with Alec's wife." Might as well admit it, since Owen was going to be entrusting them with his children. "We ran into each other while jogging, and one thing led to another."

"You're a nurse. Contraception is not exactly a foreign concept."

"The condom broke," Erica said. "Satisfied, Doctor?"

He tilted his head. "Picked an OB yet?"

"Dr. Brennan."

"Good choice," he said. "However, you don't count toward her total for the contest." Over the weekend, the press had seized on the announcement with glee, and Erica had heard murmurs about doctors forming alliances to support their favorite charities.

"I'm aware of that," she told him cheerily. "You can't count me, either. Which charity have you picked?"

"Haven't decided," Owen said. "Anyway, I'd rather not take sides."

"I don't blame you."

A few nurses entered, putting an end to the conversation. Well, she'd told her boss about her situation, Erica reflected. That was one hurdle crossed.

Later, on her way to the cafeteria after surgery, she considered the possibility that babysitting those cute kids would have an impact on her, too. Taking care of her cousins when she was a teenager had been fun the first few times, until her aunts decided to make the most of having a free babysitter. Her mother had insisted it was good practice and that her sisters deserved a break. When Erica complained to her father, he'd scolded her for acting selfish. No wonder she'd learned to hide her feelings from her parents.

With Lock, she felt safe to open up. The way he'd held her while she unloaded about her brother had been wonderfully supportive. Too bad the condom had broken.

Was that really such a terrible thing?

Yes, Erica answered promptly. But perhaps not as terrible as it had seemed at first.

Her hand drifted to her still-flat abdomen. She'd spent so many years considering pregnancy as a medical condition that she hadn't given much thought to the more profound implications. Not that she was ready to embrace motherhood. Yet sometime in the past few days, her initial panic had eased.

In the cafeteria, she approached the line for hot food. Nearby, Ned Norwalk lingered by the dessert display, his gaze fixed on her. What was he doing, trolling for gossip?

When he started in her direction, Erica tamped down her impatience. While she didn't enjoy having to guard her words around the notorious gossip, they both worked with Dr. T and they needed to get along.

"Hi, Ned." She mustered a smile.

"Can we talk?" He spoke tautly.

"Something wrong?"

He glanced around. No one appeared to be paying them any attention. "I was looking for Dr. T earlier and I happened to hear part of what you said in the break room."

With a sinking sensation, Erica recalled the footsteps in the hall. Why hadn't she noticed that they didn't continue on? The man must have heard enough to keep the entire hospital buzzing for days. An unplanned pregnancy with a man she scarcely knew, and now Ned wanted to grill her for more details? "What I said was in confidence!"

Ned raised his hands in a calming gesture. "I'll admit I'm not shy about spreading the word when someone drops it in my hot little ears, but eavesdropping's a different matter."

"Good," Erica said. "So what's on your mind?"

"There's something you ought to know. Let's go outside, okay?"

Reluctant as she was to share confidences with him, her colleague sounded sincere. Anyway, he'd already heard the worst. "Okay."

A minute later, they stood on the cafeteria patio, which was empty thanks to the nippy March breeze. Impatiently, Erica waited for Ned to explain whatever he thought was so important. Some insight about Dr. Brennan? Or a warning about Bailey's overprotectiveness toward the twins? Ned and Bailey were buddies from way back, she recalled.

His words took her completely off guard. "It's about that man you mentioned, the detective. Lock Vaughn."

Erica hugged herself, shivering. "You know Lock?"

"We've met." Ned braced himself, feet apart. "I just thought you should be aware that he came around asking questions about you."

Why would Lock do that? She'd be happy to answer his questions herself. "I don't understand."

"He questioned me about you a couple of months ago. In January."

Impossible. That was before they'd met. "It must have been later."

"No, I'm pretty sure that's when it was."

Whatever else people might say about Ned, he usually got his facts straight. "This doesn't make sense," Erica said.

"Not to me, either." He spoke quickly, cutting off further protest. "Let me explain, okay?"

"Okay," Erica said. And stood there listening with growing dismay.

Lock hadn't met her by chance. From the very beginning, he must have lied to her. It was worse, much worse, than she could have imagined.

Chapter Thirteen

Monday morning was slow, and therefore a good time to catch up on paperwork from the weekend's activities. In his office, Lock updated Phil's file with his notes from Saturday and read his email. After taking care of business messages, he checked his personal ones.

In the days immediately after he'd forwarded his information on the adoption site, he'd considered possible reasons for woman number three's silence. On vacation? Already found her relinquished son?

When nearly a week passed without a reply, he'd begun to get angry. Why didn't she bother to answer? At the very least, he deserved the courtesy of a response.

Now here it was, a reply with the same header the site had sent to all three women—Re: Your Confidential Inquiry—along with an address he didn't recognize. Lock tightened his grip on the mouse.

Finally, a step toward getting some answers. Why he'd been abandoned. Why she'd chosen the Vaughns. What had happened to his father.

Scarcely able to breathe, Lock opened the email.

The message began: If you have a diamond-shaped birthmark on your inner right ankle, then I'm your mother.

Lock's heart rate sped up. He hadn't mentioned the

mark in anything he'd posted. While it wasn't as convincing as DNA evidence, it came close.

Swallowing hard, he continued reading.

I'm 62 and in good health, except for high cholesterol. There's no medical information about your father, who's dead now. You have no brothers or sisters. That's all I can tell you. Since filling out the form, I've decided I don't want any further contact. I'm happy with my life the way it is.

This is a temporary email address. In case you have some urgent question, I'll check it again in a few days, but please don't expect anything more. Goodbye.

He stared at the screen in disbelief. This was all he got? Not even a first name, no explanations, no willingness to meet and heal old wounds. This was *his* life, not just hers. How selfish could the woman be? Obviously she didn't give a rap about his messed-up childhood. Just as she'd done thirty-five years ago, she was thinking only of herself.

Lock clenched his fists. Although he'd known any number of reactions were possible, including continued silence, he hadn't been prepared for outright rejection. In a fury, he typed a response to make sure she knew exactly what he thought of her and why.

His professional side reminded him it was never a good idea to send a message in anger. Too bad. He'd never hear from her again, anyway.

After a light tap, Sue Carrera peered in his door. "Phone call, Lock. It's a woman."

Guilt twisted through him. Had his mother changed her

mind? He'd have to apologize…except he hadn't provided a phone number or any information about the agency. "Did she give a name?"

"Erica." The secretary's eyes shone with curiosity as she awaited his response. She loved anything that hinted of romantic entanglements, as if her coworkers were characters in a soap opera. So far, the only one who'd given her any satisfaction was Patty, who'd reconnected with high school sweetheart, Alec, while guarding his five-year-old daughter.

Well, Lock supposed, sooner or later Sue was bound to learn how he felt about Erica. But not yet. "Thanks. I'll pick up."

With obvious reluctance, the secretary departed.

Why hadn't Erica called him on his cell? he wondered belatedly. The answer, he discovered when he checked, was that he'd forgotten to turn the thing on this morning. No wonder things had been so quiet.

He picked up the landline, reminding himself to keep his voice low. The office had thin walls and big ears. "Everything okay?"

"You didn't run into me in the park by accident, did you?" No greeting, only accusation.

What had she heard, and from whom? "We should get together and discuss this in person."

"Just answer the question," Erica snapped.

"Yes. No." Lock wanted to be frank but discreet. If only he'd prepared for this bombshell. "Which time?"

"Don't play games with me!" Her voice rang with anger. "You manipulated me from the start. Why?"

"Slow down." *And give me a chance to get my bearings.* "What is it you've heard?"

"You were asking questions about me in January. Before we met. Nosy, insulting questions."

"Who told you that?" Surely not Patty or Mike.

"Ned Norwalk. Male nurse. Early thirties, blond hair, blue eyes. Ring a bell?" Without waiting, she rushed on. "I can't believe the stuff you asked—whether I threw wild parties and showed up at work drunk. Oh, and was I sexually promiscuous!" She gulped as if the words stuck in her throat. Which they probably did.

"He's exaggerating." Lock hadn't phrased his inquiry in such insulting terms. *But I implied them.*

"That's all you have to say?" Hurt and disappointment laced her tone. "You set me up."

"That's not true." *What a mess,* Lock thought, rubbing his forehead. He had to find a way to straighten this out. "It's true that I didn't meet you by accident that first time. I was investigating you. But what's happened since then is another matter entirely."

"Investigating me why? For whom?"

He wished he were free to explain. "I can't breach my client's confidentiality," Lock told her unhappily. "Erica, I'm sorry. I know it sounds bad."

"I could understand checking out my reputation, although I have no idea who put you up to that," she went on. "But you tried to pick me up. What was that about?"

Oh, hell. "It was—" if only he'd listened to his better judgment and refused that part of the assignment "—kind of a test."

A shocked pause—at least, he assumed she was shocked—greeted this revelation. "You tried to pick me up to prove what a slut I am?"

This kept getting worse and worse. "Not exactly." But wasn't that the case? "I was rooting for you to turn me down."

She paused again. "You can't think that's a reasonable excuse."

"It's true, though."

"Unbelievable." Her voice broke. "So what is this pregnancy? Proof of my poor character?"

Oh, Lord, he hadn't even considered that idea. "Of course not! Everything that's happened between us was *after* I filed my...closed the case."

"Filed your report," she finished for him. "Repeating every bit of dirt you managed to dig up from the hospital gossips. Spying on me, too, no doubt. What else did you do? Snap pictures of me?"

"Uh..." He couldn't come up with an evasion. Maybe he should quit trying.

"You did!"

"Erica, it was my job." That was honest but it sounded lame, even to Lock. "It happened before I knew you."

"I can't tell who I'm angrier with, you for being such a jerk or myself for getting involved with you." Her tone verged on shrillness. "Here's the truly weird part. All these months I've mistrusted Ned, but he's the one who was truthful with me."

Lock understood her anger and disillusionment. "I'm sorry I couldn't tell you. That would have meant betraying my client."

"So instead you betrayed me," she retorted.

"Not intentionally." He wished she'd be reasonable. Or forgiving. Or simply merciful. "Look, Erica, once you've had time to think about this—"

"I don't see how I can ever trust you again. And you expect me to turn over a baby and assume that you'll keep your word to take care of it and love it, and not try to use me as your free backup?"

She had no right to make that kind of assumption. "If you think this changes my decision to raise my kid, you're mistaken," Lock challenged.

"I'll fight you in court."

"You'd lose." Wait a minute. He hated lawsuits. "Let's leave the lawyers out of this. We can work it out. Are you at home? I'm coming over."

"Don't bother. I'm so angry right now I can't even talk to you."

"Erica—"

"Goodbye." She disconnected.

He slammed down the phone. That was the advantage of landlines over cells; they landed with such a satisfying crash.

Lock checked his watch. Nearly four o'clock, which meant she might still be at the hospital, or at home or in between. He'd give her a few hours to cool off and then stop by her apartment.

The surge of resentment at her reference to the baby faded fast. It was hard to blame her for being outraged. Hell, he was kind of outraged himself at that stunt he'd pulled on their first encounter. He should never have tried to pick her up.

This weekend, she'd been sweet and loving and open about her mixed feelings. The fact that she'd agreed to babysit with him, despite her reservations, had been a promising step. Toward what, exactly, Lock wasn't certain, but he knew this much: he wanted to be around Erica just as much as he wanted his child.

That didn't mean he expected her to take on a role she clearly rejected. Still, there'd been the shimmering possibility that they could work out an agreement that suited them both. Time together, time with their child.

Now she was slamming the door. The law might give him the right to claim his baby, but he couldn't force Erica to be his friend. Or his partner in child rearing. Or his lover.

All his adult life, Lock had abandoned relationships the way he himself had been abandoned, unable to bear the intrusive demands of intimacy. With Erica it was different.

She's like me. Maybe a little too much like me.

A hard knock gave scant warning before Mike barreled in. "So you've decided to raise your kid! Did I hear that right?"

"Whatever happened to privacy?" Lock growled.

"Whatever happened to *my* privacy if you bring a baby into our house?" His brother towered over the desk.

Lock got to his feet. Even though he was six inches shorter, he felt more in control that way. "You're the one who's trying to become a father. Consider this good practice."

"Is there some universe in which that makes sense?"

Patty's blond head appeared in the doorway. "Erica's having your baby? How did that happen?"

Both men rolled their eyes.

"I didn't mean the facts of life," she grumbled. "I meant…I thought she told you to take a hike."

"Butt out," Lock said. "I mean that in the nicest way."

"You didn't tell Mike to butt out!"

"That's because he's about to be an uncle." Lock wondered how many other people had heard that loud conversation. Sue, too? How about the seniors thumping and bumping away downstairs? The way things were going, they'd be marching up here any minute to give him advice, too.

"I helped you scope her out," Patty insisted. "I even wriggled a few details out of my husband. So this concerns me, too."

"Look, we're working it out." Lock's newly activated

cell phone rang. "I'll fill you in later." The name on the readout was Mindy Eckert, wife of the missing handyman.

Mike and Patty regarded him stubbornly.

"Client," Lock said, and answered the call. "Yes, Mrs. Eckert?"

The two exchanged frustrated glances. Reluctantly, they cleared the office.

"It's Josiah!" Mindy exclaimed in a distraught voice. "He just called from Ensenada, Mexico. He has no idea how he got there or where he left his car. He sounded confused. I got the name of his hotel and promised to meet him there. Mr. Vaughn, I'm afraid he's had a stroke or something. My sister's coming over to take care of the kids, but I'm afraid to drive down there by myself."

Ensenada lay three to four hours south of Safe Harbor, not counting delays at the border. "If he's had a stroke, he should get medical attention right away."

"If he leaves his room, he might disappear again."

Mentally, Lock flipped through the possibilities. Trying to enlist the help of the U.S. Consulate or Mexican authorities would take too long if this was a medical emergency. And Mindy was understandably in no mood to wait. "Do you have a passport? What about him?"

"They're both in our safe deposit box at the bank," she said. "I checked after you asked me about that on Friday."

The guy hadn't packed with the intention of leaving the country. And while this might be some kind of trick, Josiah—based on everything Lock had learned—didn't seem like the conniving sort. "Did he ask you to bring money?"

"He didn't mention it. Why?"

"Or other valuables?"

"You think he's being held for ransom?"

"If so, he'd have mentioned it," Lock told her, and decided to take the man at his word—for now. "Get the passports, pack an overnight bag and bring as much cash as you can lay your hands on. I'll meet you at your house in an hour. I'll drive." Lock kept a change of clothing in his car, and his other documents handy.

"Thank you, Mr. Vaughn!"

"I'm just glad he's turned up."

Lock found Mike and explained the situation. "I'll look into hospitals in Ensenada and text you," his brother said. "If the man really had a stroke, you shouldn't waste any time."

"Thanks." Despite Lock's strong urge to head over to Erica's place, that discussion would have to wait. Besides, a few days might give her a chance to cool off.

As he hurried out, he wondered if he'd hear anything further from his coldhearted mother. Once she read his response, she ought to realize that she owed him more than that unhelpful email.

More likely, she'd go smugly on enjoying her cozy life. But for now, he had more important matters to deal with.

"It only bothers me when I'm lying down," Erica told Paige as she rested on the examining table. "Like now." The pain had begun this week, radiating through her legs and buttocks, then vanishing when she shifted position.

"Please sit." The obstetrician helped her up. Immediately, Erica felt better. "Are you still in pain?"

"It's gone," she said. "What is it?"

"It's called sciatic nerve pain. It's not unusual for that to appear at around eight weeks of pregnancy."

"What fun," Erica groused.

Paige smiled sympathetically. "Swimming helps some patients, and so does applying heat or cold. You can try acetaminophen if you like. Avoid lifting anything heavy, and it's best not to stand for long periods."

"I'm a scrub nurse!"

"Does it bother you while you're in surgery?" the doctor asked.

"Not yet. Will it?" Erica waited anxiously for the response. She'd figured her pregnancy might complicate her life in the last trimester, but not this early.

"If it does, try elevating one foot on a support of some kind. And let me know if it gets worse." Paige glanced at her computer screen. "Did I mention that your blood tests came back normal? Everything looks good."

That was reassuring. Another thought occurred to Erica. "Could emotional distress bring on a nerve problem?"

"I haven't heard that, but you never can tell." Concern replaced Paige's professional cheeriness. "Last time we spoke, you planned to look into adoption. How's that going?"

"I ran into a snag with the father." Erica drew her knees up to get more comfortable. "He wants to keep the baby himself. I was ready to consider it, and then I discovered he's been lying to me." She explained about Lock's occupation and Ned's disclosure. "I feel...I'm not sure what the word is."

"Violated?"

"Exactly." Violated, angry and deeply hurt. Lock hadn't even bothered to contact her since their phone conversation. She hated to admit how much she'd cried this past week. After her divorce, she'd sworn never to let a man reduce her to tears again, and here she was sobbing like a schoolgirl.

"Surely you don't think he impregnated you on purpose!" Paige sounded horrified.

Lock wasn't *that* devious. "No, no. I just wish I knew the whole story, but he claims he has to protect his client." Erica had given the matter a lot of thought, much of it during sleepless nights. Sometimes she felt a glimmer of understanding, but not enough to excuse Lock. "How could I trust him with the baby now?"

"You have another seven months to think about it," Paige pointed out.

"I suppose so."

Erica wished Lock would come see her. Despite the way she'd chewed him out on the phone, he should still realize she needed his support, so why hadn't he called?

She sighed. She'd taken up enough of the doctor's time for today. "I'm glad my pain doesn't indicate a serious problem."

"Both you and the baby are fine. If you like, we could schedule a sonogram."

The offer hung in the air, shiny and tempting. It would let Erica see her baby. In the very early stages, of course, but how miraculous....

What's wrong with me? That's the worst idea ever. "No, thanks. In the long run, this isn't going to be my baby. It will be loved and raised by someone else."

"Having an ultrasound might help you be sure that's what you want," Paige murmured.

"Or it might tempt me to make a stupid emotional decision." Erica swung her legs off the table.

Paige took her arm to steady her. "Just because a decision's emotional doesn't make it stupid."

"Don't pressure me!" Erica snapped.

The doctor raised a hand apologetically. "That wasn't my intention. I'm sorry if it came across that way. But you do seem conflicted."

"I don't see how a sonogram is going to make me any

less conflicted," Erica replied. "But I appreciate that you mean well."

"You're facing a lot of complicated issues," Paige said. "Pregnancy should be a happy time when you prepare for a baby. If only we lived in a perfect world."

"If this were a perfect world, the condom wouldn't have broken."

She hadn't meant to get cranky with Dr. Brennan, Erica reflected ruefully a few minutes later as she exited the medical building. She wished they could have talked longer. She missed having women friends.

She hadn't seen Renée this week except to say hello in the hallway, Erica realized. Why not seek her out? She ought to be getting off her shift about now.

Erica headed for the hospital. On the fourth floor, in the volunteers' locker room, she found her friend changing from a pink uniform into street clothes. One look at her drawn face and red eyes and Erica forgot her own worries. "What's wrong?"

"I've done something horrible." The older woman drew an agonized breath.

"Did you tip over a wheelchair?"

Renée's eyebrows shot up. "What? No, nothing like that."

"I've had a rough week and obviously, you have, too." Erica tucked her friend's arm through hers. "Let's go have a cup of tea and pour our hearts out."

"I'd like that." She blinked hard. "I keep turning things over in my head, but it only makes me feel worse and worse."

"Me, too," Erica said. "Your place or mine?"

"Mine, if that's all right," said Renée.

"You bet."

What could this sweet soul have done to cause such

a guilty conscience? Erica wondered on the drive to her fairy-tale cottage. The flowery decor with its fantasy figures and pleasant scent lifted her spirits, and she settled comfortably with her cup of tea. "You go first."

"Are you sure?" Renée asked.

"Shoot. I'm ready."

After taking a shaky sip, she set the dainty cup aside. "I emailed my son and told him a little about me, just some basics, and explained I didn't want any further contact. That I like my life the way it is. Don't I have the right to do that?"

"Of course." Erica understood how threatening it could be to face a total stranger with so many issues between you.

"Yesterday I checked the temporary email address I'd set up." Renée's hands tightened in her lap. "He accused me of ruining his childhood. The couple who adopted him got hooked on drugs and dumped him in foster care. All these years, I've imagined I did the best thing for him. He acts as if it were all my fault. I was only seventeen. What does he expect from me?"

With a start, Erica realized she was hearing the other side of a familiar story. Lock's story.

Renée was his mother. That made her the baby's grandmother, as well.

Now what was she going to do?

Chapter Fourteen

A pounding on his bedroom door woke Lock at a ridiculously early hour on Saturday. Blearily, he heard his brother call, "Hey, Sleeping Beauty, you've got a visitor."

"Get lost," Lock responded, in what he considered a restrained manner for a guy who'd returned from Mexico late the previous night.

By the time he and Mrs. Eckert had arrived at the Ensenada hotel on Monday evening, Josiah had gone missing again.

Lock had made a few calls that evening, and the next day they'd begun to search, eventually finding him in police custody. He'd been sleeping in an alley with no identity papers and no idea how he got there. It had taken hours to get the situation sorted out and arrange his release from jail.

Josiah had greeted his wife with relief and gladly gone along with them to a hospital, where much of the staff spoke English. Tests had indicated he suffered from very high blood pressure, which had spiked and caused his confusion and strokelike symptoms.

While he was in treatment, Lock and Mindy had crisscrossed Ensenada until they'd spotted Josiah's car parked in a dirt lot. Finally, on Friday, the doctors had released their patient to return to California, where he would seek further care. Lock and the Eckerts had meant to leave in the morning, but thanks to paperwork delays, hadn't been able to set off until last night, Mindy driving her husband's car behind Lock's.

"I don't know what I'd have done if I hadn't had you to turn to," she'd told him once they reached her house. "No matter what it costs, it was worth it."

"Let me know how he's doing," Lock had replied. "I'm glad you got your husband back." They might never learn exactly where Josiah had been during those lost days, but at least he was reunited with his family and in good hands.

Lock hadn't made it to bed until after 3:00 a.m., his injured leg throbbing from all that driving and walking. Now it felt stiff as a pool cue. He deserved a few more hours of uninterrupted rest.

Mike, oblivious to his brother's state, yanked open the door on its squeaky hinges, marched over and dragged the covers off his bed. Cool air rushed in. "Hey!" Lock grabbed in vain for the blanket. "It's cold."

"That's what you get for wearing nothing but underwear to bed." Mike dodged the pillow Lock threw at him.

"As opposed to your favorite sissy striped pajamas?" Lock groaned. "Who would visit me at this hour, anyway?"

"It's two in the afternoon."

"Yeah?" He squinted at the clock, confirming the time. "Well, I'm exhausted. Tell him to go way."

"I'll send her in and you can tell her yourself."

Her? "Who is it?"

"Erica."

His gut tightened. He'd started to call her a couple of times during the week, but a phone conversation just wasn't going to cut it. He'd planned to go see her this evening—after he figured out what to say. Which he still hadn't done.

"Who gave her my address?" Dragging himself out of bed, he pulled a pair of jeans and a sweatshirt from the closet. No chance to clean up without going through the hall.

"I asked her that," said Mike cheerfully, leaning on the door frame. "Seems she found out from Patty."

"Next time I move, it'll be to a town where nobody knows anybody." Grumpily, Lock dashed to the bathroom.

A few minutes later, still feeling gritty but unwilling to leave Erica to stew any longer, he limped down the hall to the kitchen. She sat at the table drinking coffee, and looking good enough to eat in a flowered blouse and pink sweater, her hair a soft blond cloud.

And he was starving.

"Tell me that isn't the last cup of coffee," he said.

"Not quite." Erica indicated the coffeepot, where half a cup remained. The light was still on, so at least it should be hot. Although tempted to pour it straight down his throat, Lock reached into the cabinet for a mug.

"I've been in Mexico," he rasped.

"Your partner told me."

Thick and strong, the coffee burned its way into his gut. "It was an emergency. I didn't have time to see you before I left."

"They don't have email or phones in Mexico?" Erica shook back her hair. Lock couldn't read her expression today. Still angry? Disgusted?

"I figured we should talk in person. Once I was feeling human again." He took a seat beside her. "Which I'm not."

"Too bad, because you're on the hook."

"For what?"

"This morning during surgery, Dr. Tartikoff mentioned that he and his wife bought tickets to a musical tonight. They're counting on us to watch the kids. I'll go alone if you can't make it, but you did promise."

She was still willing to babysit with him? Amazing. Thanks to the caffeine, the fog in Lock's brain was lifting. Tonight presented the very opportunity he'd been seeking, both to learn about babies and to spend time with Erica. If he hadn't felt so drained, he'd have let out a cheer. "I'll clear my social calendar. What time?"

"Seven. Is that all you have to say?" She regarded him through narrowed eyes.

"I haven't eaten anything since lunch yesterday," Lock said. "Are you going to explode sometime in the next few minutes, or can I fix myself something to eat?"

"Both."

"Any chance I can kiss you without getting bitten?"

She only glared harder.

"I could answer that for you," Mike said from across the room. He must have slipped in unnoticed. "It's no."

Lock lumbered to the fridge. "Go away. Erica and I need to talk."

His brother didn't move. "I live here."

Lock blurted the first thing that occurred to him. "I'll tell Mom."

"Okay, okay." With a shake of his head, Mike ambled back into the depths of the house.

"He's your brother?" Erica asked in confusion.

In the freezer, Lock found a chicken dinner. "Foster brother."

"What else haven't you told me?" Her voice had that telltale quaver again.

He put the food in the microwave. "Erica, I'm sorry about the way we met, but I'm glad we did."

"Ginnifer Moran hired you, didn't she?"

A denial stuck in his throat. That might be because he'd finished the coffee and badly needed more. Finally, he muttered, "I can't say."

"A friend in Boston emailed to say Ginnifer and Don broke up, and that I should check her Facebook page, so I did," Erica told him with a trace of amusement. "She calls Don a sleazeball who lied about his ex-wife. That would be me."

Thank goodness she'd figured this out without his having to tell her, Lock thought. "What else did she say?"

"That she hired a detective who proved his ugly stories weren't true. What did he say about me, anyway? That I pick up men in parks?"

"Not parks, specifically." Lock pulled her up from the chair and put his arms around her. To his relief, she rested her cheek on his shoulder. "Erica, I hate what I did. I'm glad you turned out to be the opposite of everything your ex-husband claimed, and that I was able to clear your name. You're very precious to me, and I'm asking you to forgive me. I'd seriously consider getting down on my knees, but I might never be able to get up again."

She lifted her head. "Your leg hurts?"

"Like fire. Any chance of a massage?" He stroked her hair, releasing a light, fresh scent that felt oddly healing.

"I was going to suggest ibuprofen." She drew back with a trace of reluctance. "Did you tell her you slept with me?"

"No way!" Lock took Erica's hand. "I filed my report after our first encounter. The rest is none of her business or anyone else's."

"I'm afraid it's the whole world's business now." She rested one hand on her stomach. "Everyone at the hospital must know about my pregnancy."

Well, so what? "I've missed you," he said. When the microwave buzzed, he ignored it.

"Much as I hate to admit it, I've missed you, too." She appeared to be fighting a smile.

"Pick you up at a quarter to seven. Anything special I should wear? Wading boots? Combat gear?"

Erica laughed. "You're hopeless."

"On the contrary, I'm very hopeful."

"There's something else. But we'll discuss that tonight." She got to her feet. "Enjoy your meal."

Despite the rumbling in his stomach, Lock walked her to the front door and held it open. He'd have liked to escort her to her car, but his leg really did hurt. And in his current mood and state of hunger, even a microwaved chicken dinner smelled like heaven.

Tonight. Erica. Babies. His spirits soared. As for whatever else she wanted to talk about, he'd play that by ear.

She hadn't intended to forgive him, but the sight of Lock all rumpled and repentant had gone straight to Erica's heart. Thank goodness it was a short drive home, because she had to force herself to pay attention to traffic. Her body still vibrated with the feeling of his arms around her and the earnestness in his face. Being with him had dissipated her anger and thrown her so far off track she hadn't found a way to bring up the subject of his birth mother.

Last night at Renée's, Erica had done her best to console her friend without revealing what she knew. Not until she could think it through. And the more she mulled over the subject, the more obligated she felt to protect both mother and son. But she couldn't ignore the situation, either. Renée was suffering, and Lock must be, too, or he wouldn't have unloaded the way he had on his birth mother.

Erica cared about both of them. As if the situation wasn't complicated enough, she was carrying Renée's grandchild. What a tangle!

Tonight, while they were babysitting, Erica would have plenty of time alone with Lock. Somehow, she'd find a way to tell him about Renée. And persuade him, once and for all, how foolish this single-dad business was. He'd just taken off for Mexico on a moment's notice, for heaven's sake. As for his house, how could he bring up a baby in a bachelor pad with a pool table in the den?

Even if he gave in, Erica knew it was going to cost her. Once they went through the ordeal of giving up their baby, how could they feel comfortable around each other? She was going to lose him.

And Renée, too. Once she found out this was her grand-child, she was likely to drop her hands-off attitude about Erica's decision to relinquish. But then, hadn't Erica learned not to count on others?

That reminded her of a task she'd been putting off: call-ing her mother. A check of her watch showed that it was nearly three, almost six in the Boston area. Although her mom might have plans on a Saturday night, it was early.

Nurturing might not be Bibi's strong point—she often behaved more like a sibling than a parent—but surely she'd rise to the occasion. Friends might come and go, boyfriends and husbands might disappoint, but your mother was always there. And Erica sure could use some motherly reassurance, she reflected as she dialed.

"Bonsoir," Bibi answered in a lilting tone. She'd been taking a French class in anticipation of a European tour she and her sisters were planning.

"Hi, Mom." Guiltily, Erica realized it had been weeks since she'd called. "It's me."

"Maman, s'il vous plaît," Bibi sang out. In the back-

ground a chair scraped. Erica pictured her mother, hair tinted honey-blond and makeup in place, taking a seat in her black-and-gray art deco kitchen.

"What are you up to?" Erica asked, and listened with interest as her mother described how she and her sister Lily planned, while traveling, to pick out furnishings and fabrics for their interior design customers.

"I can't wait to see the shops in Paris and Milan! And we'll be able to write off the trip as a business expense."

"I'm glad you're having fun." Erica took a deep breath. "Mom, there's something I need to tell you."

"You're getting married! I knew you'd meet someone in California." Excitement bubbled in Bibi's voice. "Who is he? Have you set a date?"

"I'm not engaged, Mom. I'm pregnant." She hadn't meant to put it so baldly. Now that she had, she might as well spill the rest. "I'm planning to give up the baby for adoption. I just thought you should know."

As she waited for a reaction, Erica wished her mother would agree to videoconference, because she'd like to see the expression on her heart-shaped face. Surprise and perhaps a little dismay, but also caring. *Because I'm still her little girl.*

A sharp expulsion of breath warned otherwise. "Isn't that just like you!" Bibi said. "So selfish!"

"I beg your pardon?" Erica replied uncertainly.

"For years I've watched Lily and Mimi dote on their grandchildren. Now I'm finally going to have one, and you're handing it over to strangers!"

A knot formed in Erica's chest. "I'm not doing this to hurt you. But I have to lead my own life."

"That's all the matters, isn't it?" Bibi snapped. "God, you're cold. You've never had much feeling for others. Even when your brother died, it hardly fazed you. You drove away your husband and now you refuse to let me enjoy my own grandchild."

The broadside was so irrational and so unexpected that it left Erica speechless. Surely her mother realized that, after Jordan's death, she'd withdrawn into her grief. As for the divorce, she'd told Bibi all about Don's cheating. "Mom, you can't mean that."

"For years I've been dreaming about the day I'd have a grandchild. You were my only hope. If your brother had lived... Well, enough about that. I don't suppose anything I say will make you reconsider."

It went against the grain to lash out at her mother, no matter how unfair the accusation. "I wish you would stand by me when I need you," Erica said. "Let's hang up now, because if we don't, we might both say things we'll regret."

Then she rang off. She half expected her mother to call and apologize, but minutes passed in silence. Probably a good thing.

As for regrets, Bibi ought to have plenty. But her mother rarely apologized for anything.

Erica longed, suddenly and intensely, for a pair of strong arms to hold her close and a deep masculine voice to murmur reassuring words. For the first time she could recall, she desperately wished for someone to lean on.

Someone who looked, sounded and acted a lot like Lock.

Chapter Fifteen

Tonight, Lock saw everything from a fresh perspective.

Take Dr. Tartikoff's low, palm-tree-shaded house on a cul-de-sac. Once, Lock's first assessment would have been that it was a great place for a party. This evening, instead, he surveyed the bird-of-paradise and hibiscus plants and wondered if they were poisonous. He'd read that toddlers would eat anything.

As they walked along the path toward the front door, he mentioned the plants to Erica. "I don't think they're dangerous," she answered. "You may be thinking of oleanders."

"Oleanders are bad news?"

"Deadly."

"How do you know this stuff?" Lock asked, impressed.

"It's written on the double X chromosomes." She rang the bell.

"Seriously?"

Erica bumped his hip with hers, or tried to. She was so much shorter that she only hit his thigh. "Of course not."

"Oh." He felt a bit foolish, but enjoyed the contact.

Owen ushered them inside, apparently unaware of a small blotch on the lapel of his dark suit. "Bailey's almost done feeding the twins."

"We'd be happy to take care of that." Cautiously, Lock glanced at Erica. "Wouldn't we?"

"We don't give them formula," the doctor answered. "Strictly breast milk. We should be home in time to feed them again, but if they get fussy, you can give them distilled water."

"Bailey doesn't supplement with formula?" Erica said. "That must be hard with twins."

"Formula affects the beneficial bacteria in their gut. Fortunately, she has enough milk. She wanted to express some in case you needed it, but her supply isn't quite *that* large." The doctor led them to the living room.

Lock eyed the heavy chairs and massive couch. "Is this special kid-proof furniture?"

"No. Frankly, it's rather old-fashioned for my taste. I inherited it from my parents."

"It's beautiful," Erica said.

"It may not be so beautiful when the kids get done using it for gym practice, but I won't mind." Dr. T slanted them an ironic grin. "Back in a sec. I better find out what's holding up Bailey."

As he disappeared into a bedroom, Lock said, "I didn't know that stuff about formula. Does that mean it's bad for kids?" He didn't see what choice a single father would have.

"No, but breast milk is better. Too bad we don't have the tradition of wet nurses anymore." Erica stayed close beside him, perhaps feeling intimidated in her boss's house.

Or maybe she felt cuddly. He hoped so. Trying to stay on topic, he asked, "What else should I know about babies?"

Erica indicated an electrical outlet fitted with a plastic

cover. "That's a safety plate so the little guy or gal can't stick a knife or a fork in the holes."

Lock flinched instinctively at the notion of an electric shock. "And, uh, why would they do that?"

"Because it's there."

Lock glanced down to see if she was joking again. She didn't appear to be.

Moving into the kitchen, Erica opened a low cabinet to display a locking device. "These help prevent poisonings from household cleaners and the like. All the same, it's best to store those things high up. Children are amazingly resourceful."

Until recently, Lock had thought in terms of external threats like kidnappers and car crashes. He was beginning to realize that kids might be their own worst enemies. He'd have to do a lot of retooling in their house, whether Mike liked it or not. "How old are they before they use common sense?"

"Eighteen," Erica said.

"Months?"

"Years. And that's a best-case scenario."

He laughed. "How old are the twins?"

Dr. T came into the kitchen in time to overhear. "Three months. At this age, the main safety precautions are putting them to bed on their backs and making sure they don't roll off the couch or the changing table."

"And keeping small objects out of reach," added his wife, following him in. A flowing green dress flattered Bailey's well-rounded figure. "We'll be home before midnight. There are bottles of distilled water in the fridge." She proceeded to give Erica instructions for warming them.

Too soon, the Tartikoffs departed. When the door closed behind them, Lock felt an unfamiliar twinge of panic at being entrusted with two helpless infants. "We should check on them," he told Erica.

"Good idea."

In the nursery, soft light picked out the images of ca-vorting teddy bears on the walls. Two cribs, one green and one yellow, flanked a chest of drawers topped by a padded tray. The scent of baby powder brought back memories of the nursery at the Aarons' house, although Lock had never lingered there. He wished now that he had.

"Isn't he sweet?" whispered Erica, peering at a sleep-ing baby. The green one-piece sleeper, complete with little feet, looked adorable—until a problem occurred to Lock.

"How do you get that thing off to change the diaper?" he asked.

"There's a panel that opens." In the other crib, a yellow-clad infant stirred at the sound of their voices. "Shh!" Erica said.

"Sorry," Lock whispered. The tiny girl's name was Julie, he recalled, recognizing the tot who'd caught his eye at the hospital auditorium. She looked so cute as she settled back to sleep.

They hadn't come here to stand around, though. "When do we start?" he murmured.

"Start what?"

"Taking care of them."

"They'll let us know." In the low light, Erica's face took on a luminous tenderness. "Watching babies sleep is the best part, my mother used to say." She turned away sharply, but not before he saw a glimmer of tears.

"What's wrong?" he asked.

"Nothing." She cleared her throat. "Let's leave them alone."

In the living room, Lock cast an appreciative eye at the large TV surrounded by gadgets. He'd be willing to bet they could stream some really good movies with this equipment and play the latest games. But not tonight.

He wished Erica would confide in him. Women liked to talk about emotions, he'd learned, and over the years Lock had made an effort to be sympathetic to his girlfriends. Why did Erica have to be so reticent?

"Tell me what's wrong," he said, drawing her onto the couch beside him.

She shrugged. "I had a fight with my mother." Her voice caught.

"Tell me about it." In his experience, that should be enough to open the floodgates.

To his surprise, Erica said, "I'd rather talk about *your* mother."

"My mother?"

"That email you sent her." She spoke quickly, as if taking a plunge. "I agree she should answer your questions, but remember, she was only seventeen. She didn't mean to ruin your childhood."

Had he told Erica about that and forgotten he had? Lock wondered. No, impossible. He'd been out of town since he'd sent the message, and when he saw Erica earlier, they'd been arguing about his investigation. "Where is this coming from?"

She made a rewind gesture with her hands. "Sorry. I got ahead of myself."

"You got ahead of me, too." How could she have found out? He hadn't confided in anyone, not even Mike or Patty. "Who told you about the email?"

"There's this volunteer at the hospital, an older woman. We've become friendly the last few weeks." Erica watched him intently. "Yesterday she said she'd heard from the son she gave up for adoption, and to my shock I realized it sounded like you."

Erica and his biomom had met? "What did you tell her?" he asked sharply.

"Nothing. I didn't want to say anything until I talked to you."

"Thanks." Although Lock had figured his mother might still live in the area, it hadn't occurred to him they might have acquaintances in common. Worse, that she and Erica might be friends. "Surely you don't think we can kiss and make up just because we both know you."

"No, of course not. But I'd like to tell her about you."

"Why?"

"Because that way she won't find you so threatening. Then you two can meet and hash this out."

Once, Lock would have seized on the idea. But after all he'd endured growing up, his mother's indifference rankled. "She made it plain she doesn't want to see me or talk to me."

"She's hurting."

"She'll get over it." He was in no mood to sympathize with the woman.

"But you won't," Erica told him earnestly.

What made her think that? "I'm already over it."

"You're thirty-five years old and you still have mom issues. I understand, because I'm thirty-one and I still do, too." Erica paused, then admitted, "Tonight my mother called me selfish and cold. All because she wants a grandchild and I refuse to spend the next twenty years doing the hard work of raising one. I guess to my mom I'm nothing but a means to an end." Her lower lip trembled.

She looked so vulnerable that Lock drew her onto his lap. "Your mother doesn't deserve you."

"You can be a real sweetheart." Erica curled against

him. "Renée, your mom— I'm sorry, I didn't mean to say her name. But Renée would adore you. She's just scared."

"Scared?" That was hardly his impression of the woman.

"I don't think it's my place to tell you her story. You should hear that from her," Erica said. "But she never imagined things would turn out so badly with your adoptive parents."

"She hasn't apologized. Or even indicated that she gives a damn." Despite his irritation, Lock was glad to be cradling Erica. Usually, touching a woman meant a prelude to sex, but tonight he understood why women sometimes simply wanted to be held. The connection strengthened and soothed him.

"She's intimidated. Apparently, your message came across as really angry and it frightened her," Erica told him. "She doesn't know you."

"How can she when she refuses to communicate?"

"I could serve as a mediator," Erica offered. "If you want, I'll arrange a session on neutral territory. Like my place."

She wasn't the type to meddle in other people's business, so Lock appreciated the effort. Still, he wasn't ready to make a decision. "I gather you and your mother need a mediator, too. I could take a crack at that."

She gave him a tremulous smile. "There's the little matter of a few thousand miles between us. And the fact that you and she are basically on the same side about keeping the baby."

"Not about your keeping it," Lock stated firmly. "That's your call."

Whatever she might have responded was forgotten when a wail issued from the bedroom. As he and Erica got to their feet, the cries came in stereo.

"Okay, daddy-in-training," she said. "Let's roll up our sleeves."

"I'm ready."

He hadn't given her an answer about his mother. *Saved by the yell,* Lock mused, and followed her into the nursery.

ERICA STRUGGLED NOT to look amused as Lock made a third stab at fastening baby Richard's diaper. She'd laughed aloud when his first attempt sent the clean diaper sliding to the floor, but subsided after seeing Lock's embarrassment. In the second attempt, he'd ripped off the adhesive tabs and had to start afresh.

Holding Julie against her shoulder, Erica watched Lock's large, gentle hands tug the diaper tighter. On the changing table, the infant had stopped fussing at last.

Catching Lock's questioning look, she reached down to check the diaper. It held fast. "Good job."

"Finally!"

She nodded toward Richard, who was regarding Lock gravely. "You've won his respect."

"I've terrified him into silence," he corrected. "What now?"

"Go wash your hands."

"Right!" After setting the baby in the crib, he hurried into the adjacent bathroom and returned a minute later in a more sanitary condition. Richard was still wide-awake. "Can I pick him up now?"

"Be sure to support his head."

Lock obeyed, taking great care. He was dead serious about this whole process, Erica had to admit. While she still doubted he understood the challenges ahead, she gave him credit for dedication.

Maybe he *could* make a go of it. As he'd said, plenty of moms did.

Something tickled Erica's neck. It was Julie, trying to suckle. "Guess it's time for the water bottle." She had mixed feelings about that. "Usually it's best to put babies back to bed quickly so they get in the habit of sleeping through the night."

In Lock's arms, Richard burbled happily. "Do we have to? We're getting along so well."

Erica wasn't eager to part with this adorable bundle, either. "You do need to learn how to hold a baby bottle."

"There's a trick to holding a baby bottle?" Dismay creased Lock's face.

"You bet." Keeping a careful grip on Julie, she moved toward the door.

A short while later, as Erica sat on the couch beside him, she was glad to see that he'd mastered the correct tilt much faster than he'd learned to diaper. "You're good at this."

"Think so?" Gazing down, he addressed the baby. "What do you think, Rich? Am I daddy material?"

The baby cooed.

"Is he named after a family member?" he asked suddenly.

"He's named after Richard Rodgers, their favorite composer. As in Rodgers and Hammerstein."

"And Julie?"

"The heroine from the musical *Carousel*."

"I'm not sure what I'll name our child," Lock said musingly. "I mean, assuming it's up to me. It seems like a huge responsibility. I'd hate for my kid to get teased for some stupid name all the way through school."

Erica's throat tightened. She knew what she'd call a little boy: Jordan, after her brother. But it wasn't going to be her decision. "Of course you can pick the name, since… if…you'll be raising it."

"You still have doubts?" He sounded hurt.

Despite her respect for his intentions, she did. "You just rushed out of town for a week. What would you have done with a baby?"

He frowned. "That doesn't happen often."

"What about getting called in unexpectedly on a weekend or at night?" Erica disliked throwing cold water on his enthusiasm, but he had to be realistic. "Babysitters aren't available at all hours or on short notice. Is your foster mother willing to serve as a last-minute backup?"

"Sometimes, I hope. When she's not traveling."

In the crook of Erica's arm, Julie stopped sucking the bottle to doze. "We'd better put them to bed."

"I suppose so." His gaze troubled, Lock arose and carried baby Richard to the nursery.

After positioning Julie on her back in the crib, Erica ran a hand over the baby's sweet little body. Jordan could be a girl's name, too, she thought.

Earlier, the babies' crying had made her breasts ache, as if they were already heavy with milk. And Julie's trusting innocence went straight to her heart.

Erica tore herself away, angry at her maternal instincts. They defied everything she knew about herself and about what was best for the child she carried. They tempted her with the idea that she might be able to stay involved, without taking on full-time motherhood, when she knew that was wildly impractical. She'd get sucked in deeper and deeper, and then be torn by guilt and resentment.

The baby deserved better. And so did she.

As HE SLIPPED out of the nursery, Lock's brain sorted through possible emergency babysitters. His foster mother probably would help when she could, but she planned to travel a lot. And he couldn't ask Patty. Not only did she work for him, but her stepdaughter was five, which meant there wouldn't be any baby equipment in her condo.

Someone ought to establish an after-hours nursery that parents could utilize. But, Lock realized, he might not trust it, in any case. A child wasn't a pet you could leave at a kennel.

He sank onto the couch, daunted by what it would mean to have a baby wholly dependent on him. His commitment to running a business with Mike meant he couldn't cut back on his hours. Even if he were still working for a law enforcement agency, he'd face rotating shifts and overtime.

Lock gazed at Erica's slightly rounded abdomen. Inside, his child was developing, becoming more complete every day. He couldn't bear to let the little guy—or little girl— down. Whatever sacrifices it took, Lock would make them.

"You never gave me an answer," Erica said from her chair. "I don't suppose there's any urgency about meeting Renée. Still, it bothers me that I'm keeping secrets from her. I mean, I'm carrying her grandchild."

The words resonated inside Lock. *Her grandchild.* "She must not have other children. She said I didn't have brothers or sisters," he murmured, recalling her message.

"That's right."

"You like this woman? She strikes you as…" He searched for the right word. "Dependable?"

"That's an odd way to put it, but yes." Erica folded her hands on her lap. "I think you'll like her."

Whatever sacrifices it took… "All right," Lock said. "I'll meet her."

"You're sure?" Erica asked.

No, but he'd do it anyway. "Set it up," he told her. "And thanks."

The woman had failed him as a parent, but she'd been only seventeen. Maybe she'd do better as a grandparent.

At the moment, it was the only option he could see.

Chapter Sixteen

That week, Erica felt like a diplomat trying to arrange a peace conference between rival nations. Who would have believed it took so much tact and persistence to bring together a mother and son?

She didn't hear from her own mom, nor did she try to contact her. While Erica disliked letting their disagreement fester, she feared they'd only argue again if they talked. Because she wasn't going to give in, and neither, apparently, was Bibi.

As for Renée, she took the news about Lock with great reticence. "He's your lover?" she asked dubiously when Erica explained the situation at lunch Monday.

"And the baby's father." Erica kept her voice low, aware that the crowded cafeteria was full of sharp ears. "I'd like to introduce you."

"I don't know what he expects from me. I can't undo the past."

"I think he wants to learn why you gave him up and what his background is. Don't most adoptees want that?" Lock hadn't explained why he'd contacted his birth mother, but it seemed a reasonable assumption.

"I'll consider it," Renée said.

When Erica relayed the conversation to Lock, his birth mother's indecisiveness seemed to annoy him. "What did she say about the fact that you're carrying her grand-child?" he asked as they jogged together on Wednesday afternoon. One advantage of his schedule was that, al-though he had to work odd hours, he was occasionally free to take breaks during the day.

"Not much." Erica had expected more of a reaction from her usually talkative friend. "She finds the whole situation kind of overwhelming."

"She should think about how it makes me feel," Lock grumbled. "I'm the kid here."

"You're a full-grown man with a temper," she retorted.

"That, too."

Did real diplomats have to negotiate with so little in-formation? Erica wondered. Did they have to answer questions with guesswork, and tiptoe around everyone's sensibilities? If so, it was a miracle peace conferences ever produced results.

At work, Dr. T thanked her again for babysitting, but tactfully avoided mentioning the pregnancy or Lock. Ned regarded Erica with open curiosity when they ran into each other, but also refrained from asking what had hap-pened with the detective. She didn't dare say another word on the matter, for fear she'd let something slip about the connection to Renée.

Fortunately, the fertility contest kept everyone preoc-cupied. Zack Sargent had proposed establishing a formal scholarship-style program to aid cash-strapped fertility patients. Although he claimed this was separate from the contest, he clearly hoped to add that hundred-thousand-dollar prize to the kitty. In the operating room, Erica noticed, he had to endure digs from Rod Vintner, who implied that Zack was just trying to assure funding for his beloved egg donor program.

By late Friday afternoon, Erica still hadn't been able to nail down a meeting for her two friends.

"It's best that we wait a while, anyway," Lock told her when he called to cancel dinner that evening. "The eleven-year-old girl you saw in the supermarket has run away from home. The police are searching, but I need to be out there, too. I keep feeling I ought to have spotted the danger signs."

"She looked angry when her uncle confronted her," Erica agreed. "But you couldn't have known."

"Maybe if her uncle and grandmother were on the same page with supervision…" He didn't finish. "Anyway, I'm going to spend the weekend trying to figure out where Kelli is. None of her friends admits having seen her, and she's turned off her phone."

"What about that guy she was with?"

"Randy claims he thought she was sixteen, and swears he's had nothing to do with her since. I'm not ruling him out, but he seems genuinely concerned. I'd appreciate your letting me know when and if my less-than-loving mother decides to spare me a few minutes of her precious time, but there's no hurry."

"Will do." Things were not looking good on the diplomacy front, Erica mused as she clicked off.

An hour later, Renée called. "I decided I'll feel better if I get this over with. How about tomorrow afternoon?"

Afraid to let the opportunity escape, Erica promised to check with Lock. And Lock, when she reached him, grumbled and growled, but finally said yes. He used almost the same words: "Might as well get this over with."

While that wasn't a great attitude on either side, Erica didn't complain. Instead, she set the time for three o'clock at her apartment.

What did diplomats serve for refreshments when they

brought enemy factions to the peace table? Something sweet, most likely. She resolved to pick up fresh-baked cookies on her way home from the hospital Saturday.

She had a craving for them, anyway.

THE RAIN STARTED late Friday night. Lock awoke several times and by 5:00 a.m. gave up trying to sleep. In the kitchen, he found his brother grumpily setting out a bucket to catch a drip in the ceiling.

"I told Leo we need a new roof," he muttered. "He's too cheap to do more than get it patched. Well, I'm calling him now, no matter how early it is."

"I'm sure he'll appreciate it." Lock had met their landlord only a couple of times. Since Mike and Leo Franco used to work together at the police department, he let his brother handle all contact. "I'm surprised it didn't bother him when he lived here."

"As I recall, we were having a drought. Now he's cozy and dry in that fancy condo." Leo had moved in with his new wife, Nora, a doctor at the med center. They lived in the same complex as Patty and her husband, with a great view of the ocean.

"Must be nice." Lock took out the coffee and measured half a cup into a filter.

"Find that missing girl?" Blearily, his brother set out a box of cereal.

"Not yet. I hope she's holed up somewhere safe."

After breakfast, he called his client, but Phil hadn't heard from Kelli. "I keep picturing her cold and wet and huddled under a bridge."

That beat some of the scarier scenarios that came to mind. "I'm going to broaden my search today," Lock promised.

"Mom hasn't stopped crying and blaming herself."

With a wry note, Phil added, "That is, when she's not blaming me. But that's only because she's scared."

It must be nice to be so close to your mother and so certain of her love that you could dismiss her complaints and accusations. Lock doubted he'd ever feel that confident with Renée. Still, he planned to do his best to put aside his resentment and give her a fair hearing. For the baby's sake, and as a courtesy to Erica.

He pulled on a hooded jacket, grabbed an umbrella and went out into the rain.

SURGERY KEPT ERICA occupied that morning, but by midafternoon doubts crept in. Why had she put herself in the middle of this situation with Lock and Renée? Either they would form a bond that included the baby and therefore excluded her, or they'd hate each other. Whatever the result, Erica thought as she waited in line at the Cake Castle bakery, she was likely to lose two people she cared about.

A little boy, fidgeting as his mother paid for their order, snatched a sample chocolate chip cookie and smeared chocolate and crumbs on his face while stuffing it in his mouth. Plucking a paper napkin from a holder, his mom deftly wiped away the worst of the damage. Despite her disapproving cluck, her mouth curved affectionately.

Erica sighed. Why wasn't she able to embrace the idea of motherhood like most women? This morning, Dr. T had operated on three patients who'd undergone years of treatment in order to bear children. *What's wrong with me?*

As the pair departed, the young male clerk regarded her pleasantly. "May I help you?"

"I'd like a dozen cookies." She pointed out her selection in the glass case. Chocolate chip and macadamia nut, white chocolate and oatmeal-raisin. They smelled heavenly.

He packaged them in a castle-shaped carton, rang up her order and thanked her for the payment.

Outside, it was pouring again. As she raised her umbrella, Erica thought of the young girl from the supermarket. Had she turned up yet? The idea of Lock searching for her was comforting, but even he couldn't work miracles.

Balancing the cookies, Erica hurried to her car.

RAIN SWEPT ACROSS the ocean, gray upon white-capped gray, as Lock drove along the Pacific Coast Highway. He'd widened his search to include Huntington Beach and Newport, showing Kelli's picture at teen hangouts and sandwich shops. No luck. He'd poked under bridges and into vacant buildings where homeless people took shelter, with the same negative results.

Lock kept flashing back to the summer he'd been twelve. Angry when the strict parents at his third foster home blamed him for a theft their own son had committed, he'd run away. He'd spent a pleasant day blending into the crowds at the beach, but after dark, he'd had to improvise. Having spent his meager funds on lunch, he'd sneaked into beach parties, scoring bits of barbecue, then slept in a car he found unlocked.

By the second day, hunger and the need to keep an eye open for the police began to wear him down. By day three, after fighting off a homeless man who tried to grab him, he'd become seriously scared.

Miserable but still angry, he'd faced the prospect of a third night with growing worry. Fantasies of being rescued by a millionaire or miraculously discovered by a Hollywood talent scout had died. Sitting on a seawall, Lock faced the fact that nobody cared what happened to him, so he had to care about himself.

Spotting a police car, he'd waved it down. Although

he'd expected to be locked up or returned to the family he loathed, he'd instead had the good fortune to be entrusted to the Aarons. Although it took years before he truly opened up to them, they'd turned his life around.

He'd been lucky. But that didn't help Kelli.

And what about his own child? Lock just knew he would make a terrific father. But what about days like this? He could hardly drag a child along on a search. No doubt his son or daughter would adapt to being left with last-minute babysitters, but kids needed to be the center of someone's attention. To know they came first.

Sure, little kids were forgiving. Not so much adolescents. He didn't want to have his own child rebel.

Was it fair to hope Renée might turn into a devoted grandmother? *And is it reasonable to expect her to fill in gaps I ought to be filling myself?*

His phone chimed. He glanced at the device and saw Phil was calling.

Lock pulled off the highway. Although he had a hands-free device, he didn't like to talk while driving in the rain. "I've had no luck so far," he said. "Anything on your end?"

A rasping intake of breath warned that the news wasn't good. "The police found an unconscious girl in Santa Ana with no ID. She's been transported to the University of California Irvine Medical Center."

"Any reason to think it's Kelli?"

"From the description—" He broke off.

The hospital was about a half hour's drive away. "I'll meet you there," Lock said at once.

"No, thanks. This is a family matter now," Phil replied grimly.

Despite being tempted to argue, Lock accepted that he wasn't part of the family. "What's her condition?"

"No word yet," his client said. "I'll let you know."

"Call if there's anything I can do."

"I will."

As he hung up, Lock saw that the clock on the dash read 3:10. He was going to be late to Erica's. Well, Renée had a warm place to wait and good company, while he'd been tromping around in the cold and damp looking for Kelli.

In no mood to call, he eased the car back onto the road.

AT A QUARTER past three, Renée finished her second cookie and pushed back her chair. "There's no point in waiting. He obviously isn't interested in meeting me."

Erica, who'd explained that Lock was searching for a missing child, didn't understand her friend's uncharacteristically snappish mood. "I'm sure he's on his way. Let me call him."

"If this mattered to him, *he'd* call *you*." Renée carried her empty teacup into the kitchen. She hadn't commented on the fact that it came from the butterfly set.

An image of herself blocking the doorway and wrestling Renée to the floor flitted through Erica's brain. Of course, she wouldn't go that far, she thought as she searched for a distraction.

To her relief, she heard heavy footsteps coming up the exterior staircase. Just in the nick of time.

"He's here," she said, and went to open the door.

AFTER THE CHILLY outdoors, Lock welcomed the warmth that met him when the door opened. The tantalizing scent of cookies reminded him that he'd missed lunch.

"Sorry I'm late. Traffic's terrible." He didn't want to discuss the latest frightening development in Kelli's case.

"Come in." Erica stepped back, her smile welcoming.

Lock glimpsed a woman across the room, behind the

kitchen counter. Holding herself stiffly, mouth pressed into a hard line. He refused to let her apparent disapproval bother him. He slid off his shoes, while Erica hung his umbrella on a hook over a plastic mat. Curlier than usual, her hair bounced as she moved.

"Wet out there," he said.

"It was wet for me driving over, too," groused the woman in the kitchen. She had a strong face with a square jaw like his, Lock noticed, and eyebrows with the same steep arch. "That didn't make *me* late."

He squelched a sharp reply. Not for her sake, but for Erica's. "I had some urgent business to take care of."

"Did you find the girl?" Erica asked as she guided him to the table, where she'd set out a plate of cookies and a pot of tea.

"It's complicated." Gratefully, Lock scooped up two cookies at once. "Thanks. These smell great."

Renée scowled. Okay, so his manners might be lacking. In his opinion, under the circumstances, that shouldn't matter.

Erica hovered uneasily. "Let me introduce you. Renée Green, this is Lock Vaughn. Lock, this is Renée."

They both nodded stiffly. Lock had a feeling that no matter what he said, it would come out wrong, so he waited until the woman spoke. Finally, she did.

"I should explain that I'm not the one who chose your adoptive parents," she said, clenching her jaw as if her teeth hurt. "I left that to the agency."

Taking a seat, Lock absorbed this information. "You had no choice in the matter?"

"At seventeen, I figured they knew best." Renée seemed to believe that closed the subject.

Perhaps it did. "I see." He tried to frame an answer, but his mind kept drifting to the hospital. To Kelli, who might have been hit by a car or attacked by someone. What about that man, an obvious drifter, Lock had talked to in Newport, the one with the nasty smile playing around the corners of his mouth? Or Randy. Lock shouldn't have been so quick to accept his declaration of innocence.

"Lock?" Erica prompted.

He dragged his thoughts to the present. After all, this was his chance to ask the question that had bugged him most of his life. "Why didn't you keep me?" he asked Renée.

"I suppose you think it's easy for a teenager to be a single mother," she said.

"It's not easy for anyone," Lock said, "but it's possible."

Erica kept looking at Renée as if expecting her to share something more. *Was there something more?* Well, the woman was sixty-two, not a kid. If she had anything to say, this was the time for it.

Renée regarded him sternly. "I don't like the way you're pressuring Erica."

"Pressuring Erica?" Lock repeated, startled.

"Renée, he isn't—" Erica began.

"I can tell how stressed you've been," she interrupted. "And look at what he just said, about how it isn't easy but it's possible. If that isn't an attempt to manipulate you into keeping the baby, I don't know what is."

"I meant it was possible for *me*," Lock explained tightly. Why had he ever imagined this woman would make a loving grandmother? Now that he'd met her, that seemed as foolish a fantasy as his long-ago dream of being rescued by a millionaire.

"All by yourself? When you can't even show up on time for an appointment with your mother?"

Anger seethed inside him at her unfairness. But he was mad at himself, too, for blithely assuming that just because he longed with all his heart to be the perfect father, he could fit a baby into his life. Phil and his mother had done their best for Kelli, and look what had happened to her. Now, Lock had to face the fact that he couldn't in good conscience raise a child alone. Thanks to the indifference of the woman who'd tossed him to the wolves thirty-five years ago, he was going to have to entrust his son or daughter's future to strangers.

The awareness infuriated him.

"Congratulations." He scooted back his chair so abruptly it nearly tipped over. "You're right. I'm not cut out to be a father. No wonder, since I come from a long line of rigid, self-centered people. But I can tell you one thing. When my child grows up and comes to ask why I abandoned him, I won't make excuses. I'll get down on my knees and apologize for failing him. But I should have known better than to expect that from you."

From the corner of his eye, he registered the shock on Erica's face. He hadn't meant to hurt her, but he'd deal with that later. Because he couldn't stay in this room one more second.

Chapter Seventeen

"I'm not cut out to be a father," Lock had said.

Erica had seen the agony in his face as the ragged words were torn from him. All these weeks, she'd done her best to persuade him to give up the baby, but success had come at too high a price. Hard as she'd fought to deny it, she loved this man, and felt his suffering as if it were her own.

Now he was rushing away. "Lock," she cried. "Wait!"

But out he went. She couldn't let me him leave in this mood. He needed to understand that they'd find a way to work things out.

"Oh, dear," Renée said. "I don't know what came over me. I sounded like my mother at her worst."

Erica couldn't deal with her friend right now. Instead, she raced through the open door, her terry-cloth slippers barely making a sound on the concrete outside.

Rain pelted her face as she ran. From around the corner she heard the familiar creak of the exterior staircase as he descended. "Lock, wait!" she cried again.

When she reached the end of the walkway, she saw his familiar figure at the bottom of the stairs, hunching forward in the downpour. "Stop!"

He didn't seem to hear. Erica started down, keenly aware of the pebbly surface of the stairs through the thin soles of her slippers. In the downpour, she misjudged a step and felt her ankle twist. *How annoying,* she thought as she reached for the metal railing.

Her hand slipped on the wet surface. A remote corner of her brain registered that she was falling. Ridiculous. Any second now she'd get a grip on the rail.

Then her legs crumpled and she slid out of control.

A SCREAM WRENCHED Lock from his preoccupation. It took a second for him to realize what was happening, and then he leaped toward Erica. But before he could get there, her head thumped the stairs near the bottom and she lay sprawled and unmoving.

"Erica!" He knelt beside her, fighting the instinct to take her in his arms, knowing it was dangerous to move her in case of spinal injury. "Honey, are you all right? Talk to me!"

A minute ago, she'd been trying to do exactly that, and he'd ignored her. Now...

Another terrible thought came to him. *She might lose the baby.* But that was secondary. If only she'd wake up.

He heard Renée's cry from the top of the stairs. "Oh, my Lord! Is she all right?"

"No." Lock pulled out his phone and hoped the rain wouldn't disable it as he dialed 911.

Reaching them, the older woman held an umbrella over him and Erica. He half expected her to blame him, as if he wasn't already blaming himself, but she just stood there.

Lock gave the dispatcher the address and answered her questions. All the while, he kept expecting Erica to wake up and tell him she was all right.

But she didn't.

HER HEAD ACHED and one side of her body throbbed. When Erica opened her eyes, she stared up, dazed. The ceiling of a hospital corridor rushed by and an unfamiliar nurse paced alongside her gurney.

"She's awake!" the nurse called to someone.

She didn't recognize the doctor, either, Erica discovered when a young man leaned over her. "Mrs. Benford?" he said. "Can you tell me what day it is?"

Erica's throat was so dry she could barely speak. "Saturday."

"Good."

She wasn't at Safe Harbor Medical. Of course not. Her hospital didn't have an emergency room.

The rain, the stairs. Falling. *Oh, no!* "My baby?"

"We've called your obstetrician," the physician said. "Dr. Brennan has privileges here, so she'll take over that part of your care."

They halted at a cubicle. Erica could hear people rushing around.

If everything was fine, why didn't he just say so? Tears stung her eyes. She hadn't wanted this pregnancy, but now...Lock would never forgive her. And her little child. She loved him or her. How was that possible?

She needed Lock. "My...friends?" she asked the nurse.

"Just let us do our job, dear," the woman said gently. "You can see your friends later."

Was he here? No one seemed inclined to tell her, and her eyelids refused to stay open.

THIS WAS HIS FAULT, Lock thought as he sat on an uncomfortable chair in the emergency room, ignoring the occasional glance from Renée. He'd always believed it was a man's job to protect the people he loved. Today, he'd failed Erica and their child.

He'd like to be able to fault the woman beside him, but

he couldn't. Why had he ignored Erica's calls? Why hadn't he seen the danger?

His phone buzzed.

On the wall, a sign warned against using cell phones in this area. Getting to his feet, he headed for the doorway while checking the readout.

It was Kelli's friend Randy. Lock had given him a business card with this number. "Lock here," he said.

"Mr. Vaughn?" The guy sounded scared. "I just got a call from Kelli. She saw on the news that the police think some girl at the UCI Medical Center is her, and she wants to let her family know it's not."

Thank God she was safe. "She's with you?"

"No. I had nothing to do with this, honest. She was ticked off at her family, and now she's scared because the police are involved. She's afraid her folks will have her locked up."

"They just want her back," Lock told him. "She won't be in any trouble. Where is she?"

"I explained you weren't a cop and that you work for her family." Randy rushed on without giving a direct answer. "She said I could bring you but nobody else, or she'll run away again. She wants an adult who can, I don't know, stand up for her."

"Serve as a buffer?" Lock glanced worriedly toward the hallway where Erica's gurney had disappeared a few minutes ago. "Did she tell you where she is?"

"No. She said she'd give instructions once we're on the way." He was breathing hard. Most likely from the fear of getting arrested. "You're coming, aren't you?"

"Let me call her uncle and then I'll meet you in front of your building."

"Thank you." He clicked off.

Damn. Lock didn't want to leave Erica, even though he

wasn't doing her any good at the moment. But how could he abandon Kelli?

He placed a quick call to Phil, who agreed to let Lock serve as intermediary. "We just saw the girl who's here, and realized it's not her," he added. "I can't tell you how relieved Mom was. She'll feel even better after she hears this news."

"How is she? The injured girl, I mean."

"They say she'll recover."

"I'll call you as soon as I know anything more."

Torn between his concern for Kelli and his fierce desire to stay with Erica, Lock went back inside. Renée met him by the door. "She's drifting in and out of consciousness. They won't let anyone see her. They're waiting for her obstetrician before they decide whether to conduct a CAT scan."

"Did she say anything?"

"She was able to tell the doctor what day it is, so that's good." Worry shaded the older woman's face. Obviously, she cared about Erica. "The nurse asked about next of kin."

Lock gave her the name of Erica's mother and contact information. She had a listed phone number, he'd discovered while researching Erica's background. "Did the doctor—" he had to force himself to finish the question "—mention the baby?"

"Only to say her obstetrician's on her way."

Lock wished he knew more about pregnancies. Erica must be about eight weeks along, which was early. Did that make the baby safer in a situation like this, or more vulnerable?

But it was Erica who mattered most. If only he could take her in his arms and beg her to forgive him.

Yet she'd made it clear from the beginning that she

wasn't interested in getting tied down. And even if she were, Lock was nobody's idea of an ideal mate. He'd proved that today, hadn't he?

"I can't stick around," he said gruffly. "I have to…" Oh, to hell with explaining about Kelli. Particularly to Renée. "I'll be back later."

Her hand on his arm stopped him. He hoped she didn't plan on scolding him again, because his patience was at the breaking point.

Instead, her stern expression softened. "I'm sorry about the way I behaved earlier. The truth is, I've felt horrible since you told me how your adoptive parents acted."

"Thanks for letting me know. Now I have to leave." Lock knew he sounded gruff, but he wasn't in a touchy-feely mood.

Renée kept her grip on him. "Your father died in an accident before you were born. I loved him." She blinked hard. "I wasn't in any shape to make plans for you, so I left it to others. I hoped you were all right, but I just wanted to put the whole business behind me."

"Great. Can we go into this later?" Lock didn't have time to serve as her confessor.

"All these years I tried not to think about you. Now I see you rushing out of here, refusing to deal with what's happened. Just like I did."

"That isn't the case at all." He resented the comparison. "I'm leaving for a reason."

"Maybe so, but please listen." Renée spoke fast, as if her life depended on making her point. "I only now realized that, because I refused to face how hurt and guilty I felt, I spent my life punishing myself. I married a kind man I wasn't in love with, and when we couldn't have children, I just accepted it. If this is the only thing I can do for you as a mother, please don't give up on Erica."

He couldn't process her remarks. Besides, he wasn't running away, he was going to help Kelli. "Thanks for the advice. Right now, I have to help a little girl."

His birth mother removed her hand. "Good luck."

"See you later."

If he knew a way to help Erica, he'd stay, Lock thought as he sprinted for his car. Instead, an eleven-year-old and her family were counting on him.

He couldn't let them down.

IN THE DREAM, Erica stood on a balcony, holding the baby as she gazed out at the ocean. "Don't get too close to the rail," she heard Lock say behind her. "Be careful with Jordan."

She gazed lovingly at the infant's face. He wore the same devil-may-care grin her brother had when he'd picked her up at the nursing school.

The railing vanished and she was falling. For an instant, Jordan's little hand clung to her blouse, until the wind ripped him away. She grabbed for him desperately, but her fingers closed on empty air. She couldn't see him anymore, and still she fell.

She'd lost both Jordans, her brother and the baby. Far above on the balcony, Lock was yelling for his vanished son....

"You need to wake up." A nurse's voice pulled Erica from the depths of sleep. She was in curtained cubicle, where monitors hummed and an IV dripped fluid through a tube into her hand.

"I'm awake." She coughed from the dryness in her throat.

"Dr. Brennan called to say she just finished delivering a baby and will be on her way as quickly as possible. She's consulting with the neurologist by phone about whether to conduct a CAT scan," the nurse said. "They're concerned about radiation."

Erica asked the most important question in the world. "Is the baby okay?"

"Dr. Brennan will examine you as soon as she arrives."

Lock ought to be here. "The father. Is he...?"

"He had to go out." The nurse didn't sound happy about that. "Your friend Renée is waiting. And we called your mother. She wants to speak to you as soon as you feel up to it."

"Not yet." Erica couldn't deal with her mother. She needed Lock. Why had he left?

Maybe it had something to do with that missing girl. Or maybe he was too upset about the baby to stick around.

Twenty years ago, she'd watched her brother's life drain from him. At some level, her father had never forgiven her for failing to prevent the crash. For all the years afterward, Erica had felt his grief like an invisible cloud around him, shutting her out.

Now she'd been careless, and she'd lost another Jordan. She couldn't begin to process how much that fall down the stairs had cost her.

If only she'd realized sooner that she loved Lock and the baby! All along, Erica had been afraid. The screech of tires, the shattering of glass. In an instant, you could lose everyone and everything you loved. Better not to take that risk. Better to lock up your heart.

Well, that had worked out great, hadn't it?

Chapter Eighteen

"So you're my shadow." Looking oddly wise, an old soul and a child at the same time, Kelli DiDonato regarded Lock across the restaurant table.

He and Randy had met her at the Sea Star Café near the harbor, where the girl asked Lock to buy her a sandwich. As she wolfed it down, Lock remembered how hungry he'd been after he ran away.

Around them, an early dinner crowd was filling up the place. Despite the warm air, Kelli shivered in her thin jacket. Long brown hair hung damply around her face.

"You spotted me?" Lock asked.

"Yeah. At the supermarket, I figured that was you who ratted us out." Kelli downed another bite. As for where she'd been the past couple of days, she'd claimed she'd hung out with some girls she'd met at a nearby college student center.

It might be true or not. In any event, she showed no obvious signs of abuse or trauma.

"I understand why it ticked you off to be dragged away, but your uncle was trying to protect you," Lock told her.

"By humiliating me?"

"If necessary," he said.

Kelli studied him skeptically. "Do you have kids?"

A stab of pain caught him off guard. For a second, Lock couldn't hide it.

Kelli's eyes widened apologetically. "You must have lost someone. Wow. You seem like this big tough guy."

"Anybody says otherwise, I'll punch his lights out." The weak attempt at a joke drew a thin smile from her.

Randy clinked the ice cubes in his soft drink. "You, uh, you said she's not in any trouble, right?"

"Right."

"And me neither?"

"I assume not." As far as Lock could tell, Randy hadn't done anything wrong.

Kelli spoke up again. "When I have kids, I'll be really nice to them. I won't yell and I'll let them do whatever they want."

"Even if it's bad for them?" Lock asked.

"Being with Randy wasn't bad for me." She turned to her friend for support.

He averted his gaze. "I thought you were older. You're a baby."

"Am not!"

"Then quit acting like one. I could have been arrested. And when you disappeared, the cops assumed I had something to do with it. Did that ever occur to you?"

"No." Kelli's shoulders slumped. "I figured my friends would be glad to have me move in, but they weren't. And now Uncle Phil and Grandma hate me."

"Are you kidding?" Lock sought a simple illustration of how much they cared. "Your uncle's paying me to search for you. He could have spent that money on himself. After all, you aren't his responsibility."

Kelli bit her lip.

"But he loves you," Lock went on. "That's the funny thing about love. It makes us put other people ahead of ourselves. We may act grumpy with them, but if they're in trouble, we'll make any sacrifice to help."

"Not like my so-called friends," she muttered, wiping her face with her sleeve.

"How about if I take you home?" Lock said.

"I don't have a real home," Kelli answered. "My dad died and my mom's all messed up."

"I understand how that feels. When I was a kid, my dad left and my mom went to prison for drugs." Lock had the girl's full attention now. "I didn't have a grandmother or an uncle. I didn't have anybody, so I ended up in the foster care system. You're lucky."

"Really?" Kelli said. "You're not making this up?"

"I'm not. That's why I'm such a tough guy."

"No, you aren't." She glanced at the menu as if she might request more food. Instead, she said, "You think they'll forgive me?"

"I think they already have."

"Okay, then."

As he put in a call to let Phil know they were heading home, Lock hoped Erica would forgive *him.* Not only for leaving the hospital, but for stalking out of her apartment and ignoring her attempts to call him back.

He supposed that depended on exactly what he'd been talking about—whether she loved him enough.

Or at all.

WHEN THE NURSE allowed Renée to visit, Erica kept the conversation short. Her head still hurt, and her friend looked tired, as well. Erica promised to call once she learned about the baby's condition.

There'd been no word from Lock. Could he be that angry with her? Or had something gone wrong with Kelli?

Erica hated to think of the worry that child's family must be enduring.

A lot like I am. She understood why Paige had had to finish the delivery before driving over here, but waiting was hard. Still, while Erica could have requested that another doctor check her, she wasn't bleeding or showing other signs of distress. Since she faced no immediate danger, and her fetus was too small for there to be any question of saving it by an emergency delivery, she might as well relax.

She didn't want to learn the bad news from a stranger. If there was bad news.

Erica's hand drifted over her abdomen. A month ago, when she'd learned of the pregnancy, she'd been horrified. Now, she had trouble remembering why she'd felt so unhappy, or why she'd been so determined to keep Lock at arm's length.

True, they'd met under such peculiar circumstances. But she no longer held it against him that he'd been investigating her, testing to see if her ex-husband was lying. He hadn't known her then.

But he does now. And I know him. That teasing smile. That rebellious hair. The habit of blinking when a remark hits home.

Erica missed him intensely. But she'd seen this afternoon, as he'd faced Renée, how raw the wounds still were from his troubled upbringing. He might not be ready for a long-term commitment and the intimacy and vulnerability that came with it. Given the strength of his defenses, he might never be ready.

At her bedside, the phone rang. Her heart leaped. "Hello?"

"Erica?" It was her mother.

Not Lock. Although her spirits sank, she tried to rally for Bibi's sake. "Hi, Mom."

"Are you all right?"

"Mostly I'm sore and bruised. I guess the nurse told you I fell on the stairs." Might as well spill the rest. "I don't know yet about the baby." She braced for a scolding. Why hadn't she been more careful…? What had she been thinking…?

"Please forgive me for coming down on you so hard," her mother said. "I can't tell you how scared I've been. I already lost one child. I couldn't bear to lose you, too."

"You aren't going to lose me."

"Don't worry about the baby. You can have more."

"What if I can't?" You never knew about something like that, as Erica had seen with Dr. T's patients.

"Then you'll live a complete, fulfilling life without children, and I'll enjoy the blessings I have," Bibi said. "I'm sorry about the things I said to you. You're a wonderful daughter in your own way."

Erica started to chuckle, and winced when the movement brought a sharp twinge. The doctor had gone easy on the pain medication because of the pregnancy, leaving her right side aching from shoulder to ankle. Her head still throbbed, although less than before. "You're a wonderful mother in your own way, too."

Bibi laughed. "Fair enough. Forgive me?"

"Of course." While they were on the subject, Erica added, "I wish Dad could have forgiven me. It wasn't my fault Jordan died."

"You think he blamed you for that?" Her mother sounded astonished.

"He could hardly face me." Erica's sharpest image of her father was of him turning away, time after time, when she got close.

"He may have said some things at the time, but he blamed himself for not finding a way to help your brother. Then you nearly died in the crash, too. He believed he'd let you both down."

"He let that come between us all those years?" she asked in dismay.

"Guilt is a powerful emotion," Bibi replied. "People with the strongest sense of responsibility are the most vulnerable. That's my opinion."

"Makes sense to me." If only she'd understood about her father while he was alive. All the same, a burden had been lifted.

The curtain around her cubicle parted. In marched Paige Brennan, pushing a cart of baby monitoring equipment. "How are you? I got here as fast as I could."

Into the phone, Erica said, "Mom, I have to go. The doctor's here." They said goodbye and hung up.

"How are you feeling?" the obstetrician asked gently.

"You tell me."

"Any abdominal pain, cramping or bleeding?"

"No," Erica said, grateful that she could honestly answer in the negative.

"Let's check you out." Paige indicated the Doppler stethoscope and ultrasound equipment she'd brought.

Erica had to remind herself not to hold her breath.

AMONG THE SCATTERING of people in the emergency room, Lock didn't see Renée anywhere. At the desk, he asked about Erica. After obtaining his name, the receptionist sent him back to a curtained cubicle.

Inside, he heard women talking, too softly for him to make out the words. "Erica?" he called.

"Come in!" her voice sang out. His spirits leaped. She

was awake and even sounded cheerful. Cautiously, he opened the curtains.

Erica lay on a narrow bed, blond hair mashed against the pillow, the hospital gown parted in front above a drape. To him, she had never looked more beautiful.

A red-haired woman in a white coat pressed a device against Erica's abdomen. It took a moment for Lock to notice the screen displaying a black-and-white cone of shifting images.

His throat tightened. "Is that the baby?"

"Yes, and he's fine." Erica seemed alight with joy. "That's him on the ultrasound."

A great swell of joy swept over Lock. *Alive. Safe.* Then he registered the pronoun she'd used. "It's a boy?"

"I mean him or her."

"It's too soon to tell." The doctor gave a friendly nod. "Hi, I'm Dr. Paige Brennan. You must be the father."

"I am." The *father*. Would he ever get used to the power and wonder of that word?

"Let me explain what we're seeing." Dr. Paige began pointing out features on the screen. As Lock studied the flickering shadows, they took the shape of a baby, curled like a seahorse. It was tiny, the features not clearly defined, yet filled with promise. His son or daughter. A little person who would grow to be a complete individual, an envoy to the future. A man who'd shake his hand and clap him on the back, or a woman who'd, well, probably shake his hand and clap him on the back, too.

"I was explaining that at eight weeks, the baby is only half to three-quarters of an inch long," the doctor explained as she slowly moved the device. "At this stage, the eyelids are beginning to form and toes are growing."

"It's…unbelievable." Lock moved closer to Erica.

"After it gets bigger, we'll be able to see only part of

the baby at one time, so enjoy this stage," Dr. Brennan told him.

"Ouch." Erica shifted on the bed.

"What's wrong?" Lock demanded, instantly concerned.

"It's sciatic nerve pain," she said.

Lock frowned at Dr. Brennan. "Shouldn't you stop whatever you're doing? It's hurting her."

The doctor didn't appear offended at his accusatory tone. "She just needs to change position, which she's done."

He felt embarrassed. "I didn't mean to overreact. Is this from the fall?"

Dr. Brennan gave a quick headshake. "It's a common discomfort of pregnancy. She and I discussed it last week."

"This is common, so early?" Lock hadn't realized pregnancy affected women at this stage, aside from morning sickness. "I thought all those aches and pains came from carrying a large baby."

"Pregnancy involves a woman's entire body. It floods her with hormones, creates an entire new organ called the placenta, and swells her blood volume. And that's just for starters."

"I had no idea." He should have been more sympathetic when Erica complained about carrying a child against her wishes. All the more reason for her to be angry with him.

She didn't look angry, though. To Lock's surprise, she reached for his hand and grasped it firmly.

The doctor pressed a button and printed out several images. "Here's baby's first portrait. Everything appears fine. The little guy was cushioned during the fall, so there shouldn't be any long-term effects."

"What about Erica?" Lock asked, his worry returning full force. "She suffered a head injury."

"When someone loses consciousness, that's always a

concern." After removing the paddle, Dr. Brennan wiped Erica's stomach with a wad of tissues. "Normally, we'd run a CAT scan, but even though we can largely shield the baby from the radiation, I don't like to risk any exposure unless absolutely necessary. The neurologist who examined her found no danger signs, such as confusion, dizziness, ringing in the ears or slurred speech. She remembers what happened during the fall, which is good."

"I'm not sure if it's good or not," Erica added wryly. "That's one memory I could do without."

Lock wasn't satisfied. "Not all symptoms show up right away." In his line of work, he'd made a point of learning about trauma care.

"That's correct." The doctor turned off the equipment. "My recommendation, Erica, is to keep you in the hospital overnight for observation. You should stay awake until bedtime and the nurses will wake you at intervals during the night. There's a neurologist on call in case you need him."

"If there are no problems, can I go home tomorrow?" she asked.

"You bet." The doctor touched her patient's arm reassuringly. "A fall like this is frightening, but you should be fine."

"Thanks, Paige."

After making sure they had no additional questions, the doctor left. Lock pulled a chair next to the bed. "I got a call about Kelli. That's why I went out."

"Is she all right?"

He explained about meeting her at the café, and that Phil and the grandmother had arrived home in time to welcome the girl with open arms. "He's going to move in with them, so she'll have a mother and father figure in the home. Kelli seemed relieved."

Erica squirmed beneath the covers. Remembering her back pain, Lock helped her into a more comfortable position. When she flinched, he released her quickly. "Are you okay?"

"Just sore. Want my advice? Go down steps the old-fashioned way. Taking a header isn't worth the time it saves."

Thank goodness her sense of humor had survived intact. "I'm glad you're okay. I wish I hadn't had to run off like that. Are you upset?"

"No, but..." She folded her hands over her stomach. "At my apartment, you told Renée you weren't cut out to be a father. Did you mean that?"

Lock wanted to shout "No!" He *was* a father. He'd always be a father. Every day of his life, he would love and care about this child. But as he'd told Kelli, sometimes love meant putting the other person first. "A man can't be in two places at once. I have to face up to the realities of my job."

"There are ways to work things out if you want to badly enough. Or have you changed your mind about that?" She watched him intently.

"If I could figure out how to be there for my child, I'd make any sacrifice." That was the agonizing truth.

"Even putting up with me?" Erica asked.

Dizziness. Ringing in the ears. Confusion. For a moment, Lock felt as if *he* were the one with a concussion. "Would you mind repeating that?"

"Putting up with me," she repeated. "As in living together, although we might have to get a bigger apartment. There are other drawbacks. I can be cranky in the morning. Also, as you're aware, my refrigerator is a disaster area. In fact, I suspect you know all my bad habits, considering that you spied on me for...how many weeks?"

"Only two," Lock replied in a daze.

She folded her arms. "Well?"

He nearly got lost in her huge hazel eyes. With an effort, he pulled his thoughts together. He had to make sure he'd heard correctly, because he might be letting his hopes get the better of him. "Have you...have you decided to keep the baby? You were so dead set against it."

"Funny how that happened," Erica murmured. "Must be those maternal hormones. I hear they keep working for twenty years, so I guess I'm stuck."

This was more than he had any right to expect. For Erica to forgive him despite his mistakes, for her to be willing to love and raise this baby when she hadn't wanted one in the first place—might this be a side effect of her fall? "You should take your time to consider this. I don't want you to end up feeling stuck," Lock warned.

She ran her hand along his arm. "I have this little problem. I've fallen in love with you. Both of you. What do you think?"

Living together. Waking up every morning with Erica in his arms and a baby beside them in a crib. All his adult life, Lock had felt walls closing in at even the whisper of commitment. Now, it sounded like heaven. "I love you, too. Both of you. Forever."

"No one can guarantee forever," Erica cautioned.

She was wrong about that. "I can't guarantee that we'll float on a cloud of bliss for the rest of our lives," Lock conceded. "I'm talking about the real kind of love, where we talk and listen and accept each other. I grew up with rotten examples of parenting and marriage, but I saw what they can be like when I went to live with the Aarons."

"My parents weren't exactly a shining example of how to communicate." She regarded him anxiously. "I still have a lot to learn."

"We'll be learning as long as we live," Lock said with growing certainty. "How to trust each other, and how to be trustworthy. But we've come a long way, and we're ready for more than just moving in together. Marry me, Erica."

Her mouth quivered. "I… This is a big decision. What's wrong with sharing an apartment first?"

Lying there in a hospital bed, she looked pale and fragile. Was he pushing too hard? Lock wondered. She'd taken a huge step already, accepting motherhood, inviting him to share her home.

Maybe he was asking too much. But he wanted them to be a family. How could either of them accept less? "We need to be one hundred percent committed. Otherwise it's too easy to get scared and withdraw. We have to know that the other person will always be there for us."

"Marriages can fail." Judging by her hesitant expression, she must be thinking of her lying, cheating ex.

"Sure, if you marry a jerk." Drily, Lock added, "I've been accused of being one myself, but I assure you, that's entirely in the past."

"Did I really call you a jerk?" Erica smiled. "I guess I did. But…there's just one thing."

He frowned, unsure what he'd overlooked. "What's that?"

"You have to agree to name the baby Jordan."

That had been her brother's name, he remembered. "Naturally," Lock said. "If it's a boy."

"Or a girl."

She was right. The name would work either way. "I'll name it McGillicuddy or Woozer if it means you'll marry me."

"Just Jordan."

"Absolutely."

Erica beamed as if a new day had dawned across the earth. "It's a deal."

"Done?" he pressed, just to be sure.

"Done."

Lock high-fived her. Then he gently slid his arms around his bride-to-be and kissed her.

Chapter Nineteen

Sheer happiness carried Erica through what would otherwise have been a less-than-pleasant night. Nurses repeatedly disrupted her sleep and every nerve cell in her body protested the slightest movement.

She experienced no confusion or dizziness, but her brain buzzed all the same. She was going to marry Lock. How amazing. How incredible.

How terrifying.

Old fears nagged at the edges of Erica's thoughts. But with the aid of mild pain medication, she dispelled them. On Sunday morning, she arrived home still cheerfully—if disbelievingly—contemplating her future with the devoted man beside her.

After settling her on the couch, Lock fixed sandwiches for them both. Why, Erica thought, had she tried to discourage him that first day in the park? How could she have resisted his blazing blue eyes, those powerful arms and shoulders and all that tenderness? But of course, she hadn't known him then.

She hadn't tasted his cooking, either. The man had a gift for assembling cold cuts, cheeses, tomatoes and bread rich with seeds and sprouts into a meal fit for a king and queen.

He was almost too good to be true.

The feeling of unreality persisted all day. Bibi was ecstatic on learning of the engagement. Erica, who'd spoken to her only long enough on Saturday night to provide reassurance about the baby, couldn't believe how her mother showered her with praise, as if Erica had won a Nobel Prize.

"I'm just getting married," she told her.

"Yes! My only daughter is getting married!" Bibi exclaimed. "And having a baby! When's the wedding?"

"Soon." Erica couldn't think that far ahead.

That evening, Renée joined them for supper, which the older woman insisted on bringing from Papa Giovanni's Italian restaurant. This time, there was no arguing. She and Lock talked quietly, at ease with each other, like soldiers who'd survived a battle and become comrades for life. They agreed to take a DNA test, just to make sure.

Erica doubted that was necessary. In the glow of the Tiffany-style lamps, she could see the resemblance in the set of their jaws, the arch of their eyebrows and the breadth of their foreheads. Would Jordan look like that, too? Her palm fluttered to her abdomen. She hoped he or she could feel the flood of loving hormones.

And that this felt real to him, because it still didn't to her.

On Monday, following Paige's advice, Erica took a sick day, while another nurse filled in. Dr. T called three times to check on her. Each time, he sounded slightly more frazzled. Finally, he asked the question that had obviously been on his mind: "When are you coming back?"

"Tomorrow," Erica said.

"You're sure you'll be well enough?" An eager note made it clear he was asking only out of guilt. Well, maybe a little concern, too.

"Yes. I hate missing the action," she told him.

"Great!" He sighed. "Why can't other nurses figure out what I want the way you do?"

"We're on the same wavelength, professionally speaking," Erica replied. "But I'm sure my sub's been fine."

Owen muttered good-naturedly before wishing her well and hanging up.

On Tuesday, Ned came in to work early to welcome her back, bringing pastries for the surgical staff. "I dread the day you go on maternity leave," he said when they had a private moment. "Dr. T nearly bit my head off yesterday for no good reason. Apparently he had a rough morning."

"He'll get over it." Still, Erica was glad Owen needed her. "Besides, I don't plan to stay away long." She'd heard that the hospital's day-care center took excellent care of infants and made arrangements for nursing mothers.

All week, she kept running into staff members who asked about her health and congratulated her on the engagement. Erica hadn't realized how many friends she'd made in the past year.

Renée met her for lunch as often as they could coordinate their schedules. With Erica's permission, she'd begun asking around about wedding facilities. There'd been quite a few weddings among the staff, so her list grew longer by the day.

Lock and Renée's DNA test came back a match. The three of them visited Lock's father's grave and left flowers.

A few days later, when Erica met the Aarons, they welcomed her warmly into the family. Lock's foster parents were down-to-earth and fun to be around.

It was too easy. Too perfect. Any minute, Erica kept thinking, the roof was going to fall in.

Nearly two weeks after her accident, on a Friday, it did. Literally.

Lock called to cancel meeting her for dinner. "We've got a big hole in the roof over the garage."

"I thought you patched that." She recalled him mentioning the problem earlier.

"That was in the kitchen." He sounded grumpy, which was understandable, since he'd had to rescue some tools and other stored equipment from the deluge. "Leo's saying he might just patch this one, too, and sell the place rather than bother putting on a new roof."

"That seems extreme." She stretched her legs along the couch.

"A lot of things need fixing around here and he's tired of being a landlord." Lock's voice warmed. "It's lucky I'm planning to move in with you. Of course, as you mentioned, we'll need a larger place."

"I'd rather raise a family in a house than an apartment," Erica mused. "If they weren't so expensive, I'd love to be a home owner." Out of the blue, an idea hit her. A crazy, bold idea. "Wait a minute. If your landlord doesn't fix up the place, he won't be able to sell it full price."

A short pause followed. She knew what Lock was mulling over, because, she'd discovered, they tended to think along the same lines.

"I have some money left from an inheritance," he said. "How about you?"

"I have savings," she said. "I'm not sure if there'll be enough, though. We'll have to make repairs, pay for the wedding and prepare for the baby."

"Let's do the math and find out."

There was enough, by a narrow margin. They agreed on a reasonable price with Leo and opened escrow on the house. Mike griped about the prospect of being kicked out to make room for the lovebirds, especially since he wouldn't be able to use his noisy exercise equipment in an apartment. They assured him he could stay for an extra month or so until he found a house to rent and a roommate to share expenses.

And so, by the following week, Erica was going to have not only a husband and a baby, but a house, too. Even the roof caving in hadn't spoiled the scenario. She wondered if she would ever feel this was true life instead of a dream.

"You'll get your feet on the ground," Lock assured her on a Saturday afternoon when she shared her thoughts with him.

"I wish I had your ability to take things in stride," she said while eating a yogurt at the kitchen counter.

Standing across from her, Lock grinned. "Is that what I do?"

She pinpointed what, to her, seemed to be the main issue. "You seem able to feel in control. To me, everything's spinning too fast."

Lock came around and massaged her back. "That's understandable. You're planning a wedding and carrying a baby." One hand strayed to her stomach. "Ten weeks. Nearly the end of the first trimester. We may be able to tell the gender soon." He'd been researching fetal development on the internet.

"I should start planning the nursery." She'd received suggestions from Bibi, who every few days emailed her links to websites and articles. "I'm looking forward to it but at the same time there's so much to consider."

Strong arms surrounded her. "What do you usually do when you feel out of control?"

"In extreme cases, I go shopping for antiques," Erica responded wistfully. "But we have to be careful about expenses."

"It doesn't cost anything to browse."

She supposed he was right. "Will you come with me?"

"To an antiques store?" Lock's expression, when she turned to face him, hovered on the edge of dismay. Quickly, he manned up. "If it will make you happy, I'm all for it."

What a guy, Erica thought, and gave him a hug.

A short time later, they arrived at A Memorable Décor. The window display had changed from a kaleidoscope of quilts to an array of rosy-cheeked china dolls lovingly outfitted in Victorian clothing. "They specialize in dolls?" Lock asked dubiously as he pushed open the door.

"Oh, that's just the current display." As bells tinkled, Erica made her way inside, stepping around a middle-aged man and woman who were inspecting a lacquered chest. The store was more crowded than when she'd last visited, but then, that had been on a weeknight.

Lock zeroed in on an oak rolltop desk that Erica hadn't seen before. Tall and equipped with cubbyholes and assorted drawers, it dominated one corner. "Look at the workmanship. I'll bet there are secret compartments."

"Spoken like a detective," she teased.

He spotted the price tag. "It costs…ouch. Well, it's fun to window-shop, anyway."

"Yes, it is. Some things just don't show up as well on the internet." Erica ran her hand over a mosaic-tiled tabletop.

They wandered along the aisles, enjoying the uniqueness of each piece. While they'd bought the house complete with contents, that didn't mean much, considering the sorry state of everything except the pool table. Erica would have to augment her furniture eventually. Not yet, though. Not at these prices.

Something was missing. She didn't realize what until the smartly dressed saleslady approached to ask if she could help.

"Did you sell the crib?" Erica asked.

Lock cocked his head. "Crib?"

"I just remembered it," she explained. "There were butterflies carved into the headboard."

"A couple asked us to hold it for them, so I moved it to the back," the woman said. "They called this morning and said they'd changed their minds."

Probably decided it was too expensive. Erica wished she'd checked the price last time, but she hadn't been in the market for a crib.

"So where is this thing of beauty?" Lock asked.

"Follow me." The saleswoman threaded through the aisles to the rear of the store. Pulling aside a curtain, she revealed a small storage area.

The burnished wood of the crib gleamed as if bathed in radiance. In the headboard, butterflies stretched their wings, delicate reminders of an unknown creator who'd surely made this lovely thing for his or her own child.

Erica could hardly breathe. "It's gorgeous."

"Striking," Lock agreed. "Of course, it would be a shame to use it only once." He slanted her a teasing grin.

"That remains to be seen," Erica returned tartly. *But he might be right. Once you have a child, why not two or three?*

"It meets all the latest safety standards," the saleslady said. "And butterflies are my favorite theme for baby furniture. They're such a delightful symbol of new birth."

New birth. Or rebirth, Erica thought. How perfect.

In a flash, she understood why she'd had so much trouble adjusting to changes that were, after all, dearly welcome. She wasn't only carrying a new life, she was starting one. Now the railing of this crib gave her something solid to hold on to as she emerged from her familiar cocoon into a new world. A world she suddenly felt ready to enter with wings spread wide, like those butterflies.

"It goes with your stuff," Lock observed.

"It does." Erica turned the price tag so she could read it. *Too much.* Her spirits plummeted.

Then she remembered the birthday gift certificate in her purse. Also, her aunts had sent a check as an engagement present, suggesting it be used to buy something for her new home. Questioningly, she turned to the man she loved. "Would you mind if I…?"

He didn't wait for her to finish. "You bet."

"I'm not sure we can afford it."

"You'll never be satisfied with anything less." Quickly, he added, "Neither will I."

Erica swallowed. "Yes," she whispered.

"We can have that delivered," the saleslady said. "Unless you want to take it with you?"

"Delivered would be fine," Lock told her.

As she paid, Erica kept touching the velvety wood, picturing an infant nestled here. And a toddler, standing shakily as it gripped the rail.

What was it that Renée had said when they first saw this crib? "It's the kind of heirloom that gets handed down from generation to generation."

A delicious shiver ran through Erica. She felt as if she'd joined hands with uncounted ancestors, women like her reaching back into distant ages. And ahead, into the future.

There were going to be more generations in her family, after all.

ON MONDAY IN the operating room, Dr. T described how Julie had begun to explore different tempos as she shook her rattle, no doubt a sign of budding musical genius, while Richard cooed along as if trying to sing.

"We're going to be like the von Trapp family in *The Sound of Music*," he chortled.

"I can't wait to see you all climbing over the Alps as you flee the Nazis," Rod Vintner grumbled.

"We bought the perfect crib!" Erica had scarcely been able to contain this piece of urgent news, and now it burst forth. "That gift certificate you gave me to the antiques store really helped. Thanks."

"What does it look like, exactly?" Dr. T asked.

"Yes, don't spare us any excruciating details," the anesthesiologist muttered.

"It meets all the current safety standards," Erica told them, and went on to describe the butterflies and how the wood shone as if with its own special light.

"He'll love it," Dr. T said when she finished. "Or she. Any idea which it is?"

"Not yet," Erica told him.

"Be sure to let me know when you find out," the surgeon told her as he bent over the patient. "Babies are fascinating."

Erica ignored Rod's grunt of disapproval. Perhaps one of these days he'd change his mind. After all, how could anyone not love those enthralling little people?

Babies. Honestly!

* * * * *

HEART & HOME

Heartwarming romances where love can
happen right when you least expect it.

COMING NEXT MONTH
AVAILABLE MARCH 13, 2012

#1393 COWBOY SAM'S QUADRUPLETS
Callahan Cowboys
Tina Leonard

#1394 THE RELUCTANT TEXAS RANCHER
Legends of Laramie County
Cathy Gillen Thacker

#1395 COLORADO FIREMAN
Creature Comforts
C.C. Coburn

#1396 COWBOY TO THE RESCUE
The Teagues of Texas
Trish Milburn

You can find more information on upcoming Harlequin® titles,
free excerpts and more at www.HarlequinInsideRomance.com.

HARCNM0212

REQUEST YOUR FREE BOOKS!
2 FREE NOVELS PLUS 2 FREE GIFTS!

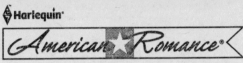

♦ Harlequin®

American ★ Romance®

LOVE, HOME & HAPPINESS

YES! Please send me 2 FREE Harlequin® American Romance® novels and my 2 FREE gifts (gifts are worth about $10). After receiving them, if I don't wish to receive any more books, I can return the shipping statement marked "cancel." If I don't cancel, I will receive 4 brand-new novels every month and be billed just $4.49 per book in the U.S. or $5.24 per book in Canada. That's a saving of at least 14% off the cover price! It's quite a bargain! Shipping and handling is just 50¢ per book in the U.S. and 75¢ per book in Canada.* I understand that accepting the 2 free books and gifts places me under no obligation to buy anything. I can always return a shipment and cancel at any time. Even if I never buy another book, the two free books and gifts are mine to keep forever.

154/354 HDN FEP2

Name	(PLEASE PRINT)

Address	Apt. #

City	State/Prov.	Zip/Postal Code

Signature (if under 18, a parent or guardian must sign)

Mail to the **Reader Service:**
IN U.S.A.: P.O. Box 1867, Buffalo, NY 14240-1867
IN CANADA: P.O. Box 609, Fort Erie, Ontario L2A 5X3

Not valid for current subscribers to Harlequin American Romance books.

Want to try two free books from another line?
Call 1-800-873-8635 or visit www.ReaderService.com.

* Terms and prices subject to change without notice. Prices do not include applicable taxes. Sales tax applicable in N.Y. Canadian residents will be charged applicable taxes. Offer not valid in Quebec. This offer is limited to one order per household. All orders subject to credit approval. Credit or debit balances in a customer's account(s) may be offset by any other outstanding balance owed by or to the customer. Please allow 4 to 6 weeks for delivery. Offer available while quantities last.

Your Privacy—The Reader Service is committed to protecting your privacy. Our Privacy Policy is available online at www.ReaderService.com or upon request from the Reader Service.

We make a portion of our mailing list available to reputable third parties that offer products we believe may interest you. If you prefer that we not exchange your name with third parties, or if you wish to clarify or modify your communication preferences, please visit us at www.ReaderService.com/consumerschoice or write to us at Reader Service Preference Service, P.O. Box 9062, Buffalo, NY 14269. Include your complete name and address.

Get swept away with author

CATHY GILLEN THACKER

and her new miniseries

Legends of Laramie County

On the Cartwright ranch, it's the women
who endure and run the ranch—and it's time for
lawyer Liz Cartwright to take over. Needing some help
around the ranch, Liz hires Travis Anderson, a fellow
attorney, and Liz's high-school boyfriend. Travis says
he wants to get back to his ranch roots, but Liz knows
Travis is running from something. Old feelings emerge
as they work together, but Liz can't help but wonder
if Travis is home to stay.

Reluctant Texas Rancher

Available March
wherever books are sold.

New York Times *and* USA TODAY *bestselling author*
Maya Banks presents book three in her miniseries
PREGNANCY & PASSION.

TEMPTED BY HER INNOCENT KISS

Available March 2012 from Harlequin Desire!

There came a time in a man's life when he knew he was well and truly caught. Devon Carter stared down at the diamond ring nestled in velvet and acknowledged that this was one such time. He snapped the lid closed and shoved the box into the breast pocket of his suit.

He had two choices. He could marry Ashley Copeland and fulfill his goal of merging his company with Copeland Hotels, thus creating the largest, most exclusive line of resorts in the world, or he could refuse and lose it all.

Put in that light, there wasn't much he could do except pop the question.

The doorman to his Manhattan high-rise apartment hurried to open the door as Devon strode toward the street. He took a deep breath before ducking into his car, and the driver pulled into traffic.

Tonight was the night. All of his careful wooing, the countless dinners, kisses that started brief and casual and became more breathless—all a lead-up to tonight. Tonight his seduction of Ashley Copeland would be complete, and then he'd ask her to marry him.

He shook his head as the absurdity of the situation hit him for the hundredth time. Personally, he thought William Copeland was crazy for forcing his daughter down Devon's throat.

Ashley was a sweet enough girl, but Devon had no desire

to marry anyone.

William had other plans. He'd told Devon that Ashley had no head for the family business. She was too softhearted, too naive. So he'd made Ashley part of the deal. The catch? Ashley wasn't to know of it. Which meant Devon was stuck playing stupid games.

Ashley was supposed to think this was a grand love match. She was a starry-eyed woman who preferred her animal-rescue foundation over board meetings, charts and financials for Copeland Hotels.

If she ever found out the truth, she wouldn't take it well.

And hell, he couldn't blame her.

But no matter the reason for his proposal, before the night was over, she'd have no doubts that she belonged to him.

What will happen when Devon marries Ashley?
Find out in Maya Banks's passionate new novel
TEMPTED BY HER INNOCENT KISS
Available March 2012 from Harlequin Desire!

Harlequin *Presents*

USA TODAY bestselling author

Carol Marinelli

begins a daring duet.

THE SECRETS *of* XANOS

Two brothers alike in charisma and power;
separated at birth and seeking revenge…

Nico has always felt like an outsider. He's turned his back on his
parents' fortune to become one of Xanos's most powerful exports
and nothing will stand in his way—until he stumbles
upon a virgin bride….

Zander took his chances on the streets rather than spending another
moment under his cruel father's roof. Now he is unrivaled in
business—and the bedroom! He wants the best people around him,
and Charlotte is the best PA! Can he tempt her
over to the dark side…?

A SHAMEFUL CONSEQUENCE
Available in March

AN INDECENT PROPOSITION
Available in April

HP13053